Baronne Staffe

My lady's dressing-room

Baronne Staffe

My lady's dressing-room

ISBN/EAN: 9783337119539

Printed in Europe, USA, Canada, Australia, Japan

Cover: Foto ©Andreas Hilbeck / pixelio.de

More available books at **www.hansebooks.com**

My Lady's Dressing Room

ADAPTED FROM THE FRENCH OF THE

BARONNE STAFFE

WITH INTRODUCTION AND ADDITIONS

BY

HARRIET HUBBARD AYER

———

NEW YORK

CASSELL PUBLISHING COMPANY

104 & 106 FOURTH AVENUE

PREFACE.

THE Baroness Staffe has written this book for French women. I have translated it and adapted and edited it for the women of America. If there were virtue in plainness, the world ought to be very much better than it is ; but the classic proverb to the effect that "Comeliness recommends Virtue" is true. Mortals are led by appearances, and the more beautiful good women are, the better equipped they will be to guide aright a world whose future depends upon the worth of its mothers and daughters.

The devout and ardent Chatelaines

of the Middle Ages felt this when they interleaved their Books of Hours with prayers and toilet recipes alternately, using one as religiously as the other.

In every age personal refinement has marked the highest stage of luxury and intelligence, and the advancement of women is one of the most striking facts of the renaissance of the last decades of the nineteenth century. One of the triumphs of our sex is that by legitimate means we have learned to care for ourselves physically, so that the spendidly-developed woman of to-day has driven the languishing invalid of our mothers' time out of existence and made her as ridiculous as she deserves to be. We have learned how not to grow old, and we have learned that with fastidious care there is no excuse for an ugly woman, and that we may preserve the beauty of youth, or a delightful resemblance to it, far past the terrible middle age which we formerly so dreaded.

I hope American women may find in this little book some hints and suggestions which will help them to maintain the charm and grace and beauty which have made them famous in the Old World as well as in the New.

Harriet Hubbard Ayer

New York,
January 1892

CONTENTS.

PART FIRST.

PART SECOND.

CONTENTS.

PART THIRD.

My Lady's Dressing Room.

Woman's Sanctuary.

" But, sweetheart, I do implore secrecy."

In every woman's home there is at least one room which bears the stamp of individuality, fashioned after her own nature, moral and physical.

If her tastes are literary, this room may be her study, where she lives an intellectual life; where she receives only her dearest and most sympathetic friends; if domestic, her own apartment, wherein are centered her tenderest maternal and conjugal interests. But the Holy of Holies is my lady's dressing room, where the profane are not admitted, from which are excluded even her *dearest ;* in which the ignorant suppose that she admiringly contemplates her perfections like some Buddha of the Hindoo heavens, or others imagine that she devotes herself to the practice of sorcery in order to remain so amazingly young and pretty; where she undoubtedly lays plans for charming and retaining her captives, through the cultivation of her physical beauty.

This room reveals the woman as she truly is, whether her object in preserving her beauty be the mere gratification of her vanity, or the more praiseworthy ambition of retaining her husband's admiration and affection. It may be luxurious and yet remain chaste as the thoughts of a young girl; or simple, and yet belong unquestionably to the most frivolous of coquettes. Here the woman asserts herself, and here her true nature, whatever it may be, is shown. Serious and trifling women must alike comprehend the importance of the perfect care of the body if they would remove or lessen the defects with which they were born.

I do not here refer to those women who crave to be universally adored, who dream of having their chariots drawn by crowds of worthless men whom a single glance enthralls, of those women who, misled by a perverted desire to please, borrow their power from empirical secrets, and so assuredly walk toward a premature old age and total loss of beauty. Neither do I wish to penetrate into the sanctuary of the false and unworthy.

I speak only of the true woman who is anxious to retain her husband's love, who aspires, and rightfully, to remain attractive in his eyes. With this object in view, if it is coquetry for a woman to use all legitimate means for retaining her youth and beauty, then it is a rational coquetry. She who understands such coquetry has listened to the divine injunction, "Adorn thyself, remain beautiful that thou mayest delight the eye and heart of the man who is the support of thine adorable weakness, and with whom thou art to continue the long line of thine ancestors. It is thy mission to please and to charm. Thou art the ideal in the hard life of man. Descend not from thy pedestal."

The clever woman, who is also a loving and loyal wife, does not permit

even her husband to cross the thresh-
hold of her dressing room while engaged in the mysteries of her toilet.
Not that she has anything criminal to
conceal, but because one can never escape from the fatal realisms of the
toilet, however beautiful, poetical,
graceful, one may be. For example—
a woman crimping her hair does
not appear to advantage, and may
even appear ridiculous. Besides, the
trivialities of life always cause us to
lose some of our prestige in the eyes
of those who love us most. Therefore, let us not obtrude the prosaic
things of life on the attention of those
whom we most desire to please. It is
unnecessary to remind the wise of
our sex that, though in certain hours
we may be goddesses, at other times
we are only like all other women.

The beauty of a woman and the beauty of a flower should be alike to man, the gift of God and Nature. It is not for him to question the innocent means used for preserving these charms.

Is it not strange that we are willing to assume a thousand cares and responsibilities, that we submit to all sorts of restraint and restrictions to build up a fortune, that we take such pains to please the most superficial acquaintance, that we strive even for the admiration of those unknown to us, and yet hesitate at any cost to hold forever the love and admiration of those nearest and dearest to us?

Some women will say that marriage is a mere slavery. I reply that carelessness and general indifference are the causes of much marital unhappiness.

Look frankly at the matter from this point of view and I feel certain you will agree with me that any sacrifice of ease or time is well worth while.   The practice of the methods I suggest will not be difficult, and I feel sure you will derive much profit from the counsel given you in this little book.

I cannot understand how a rather stout woman with over-developed legs and swollen ankles could be so cruel to herself as to walk about before her husband in a short skirt.   After presenting such a spectacle she can scarcely feel surprised that his eyes follow the graceful undulations of the lithe and supple form of a tall, slender woman.

I have seen a young woman tie her

scant and short hair with a greasy ribbon, in such a way that it resembled a hideous little tail, or small broom. Afterward she complained of the admiration her husband expressed in gazing at a head of long and abundant hair.

And so, my friends, it is right to hide our imperfections. There is no falsehood in it; we do not expect our dearest foes to expose their weaknesses. A woman who is indifferent regarding her own appearance cannot hope to preserve the admiration of her husband. On these points man loves to be deceived, and he is right. What is life, what is love, without illusion?

I am tempted to say that the other half of humanity knows even less than the fair sex, how to preserve the prestige with which a *naïve* young girl invests her first love, and that a man's thoughtlessness, under such circumstances, is utterly culpable.

One should always take as much pains to preserve as to obtain. This refers equally to present and future happiness, and to natural gifts as well as to acquired ones.

I am convinced that the ideas presented in this book will be useful to all good women who wish to be happy, and to render others happy.

The stronger sex will also find, I trust, more than one hint which will prove profitable, for, though the tyrant man must not cross the threshold of the feminine sanctuary, yet I have penetrated into the retreat where, though he pretends to be devoid of

vanity, he secretly worships Adonis.
I can but approve the care he bestows
on less delicate charms, which, however,
have their own value and are the gifts
of generous Nature.

BARONESS STAFFE.

MORSANG-SUR-ORGE.

THE DRESSING ROOM.

ITS FURNISHING.

" With everything that pretty is
My lady sweet, arise."

THE dressing room of a fashionable woman should be as tasteful and comfortable as her social position and fortune permit : simply comfortable if she cannot afford luxury, but supplied at least with all things necessary and useful to a careful toilet.

In the chapter devoted to the ceremony of the bath I give a description of the room in which the bath is taken, but here I devote myself to the dressing room proper.

The titled ladies of the eighteenth century, who enjoyed only limited opportunities for their ablutions, had their dressing rooms painted by Watteau, Boucher, Fragonard, etc., and it was here that they received their friends while they were being powdered, painted, and patched. We are too practical to expose delicate and exquisite works of art in this way to the steam and dampness of a room where both cold and hot water are used abundantly.

The walls of some dressing rooms are covered with tiles in blue, pink, or sea-green. This produces a light, pleasant effect, but is somewhat cold to the eye. Generally draperies are preferred. These should be of neutral or delicate tints, in order not to conflict with the colors of the toilet. Frequently light or bright silks are covered with thin muslin in order to soften their tone and at the same time preserve their texture.

Walls also may be covered with large figured cretonnes, or Jouy linens, but linen or cotton fabrics are always more or less cold and hard, and their large, gaudy designs often interfere seriously with the proper effect of my lady's gown, that is to say, prevent its being the prominent spot on which the light falls and to which the eye is attracted.

I prefer a dressing room in which the principal color is a pale blue, or pink, or yellow, with draperies of figured muslin. These hangings, which harmonize with any colors of the toilet, may be held back by knots of ribbon.

The floor should be covered by a rug of delicate color. From the ceiling should hang a chandelier to be lighted for the evening toilets, its candles securely forced into bobêches of colored crystal as a protection against dripping wax. This dressing room must be well lighted. The windows, of unpolished glass, may be ornamented with pretty designs and draped in silk and muslin, bordered with lace.

Indispensable Accessories.

There should be two dressing tables, facing each other, different in dimensions, but identical in form.

The larger serves for the minor ablutions. It is provided with a water pitcher and bowl of porcelain, crystal, or silver, selected with the taste which distinguishes us in these days. The dressing table is draped like the walls.

Above it fasten a little shelf on which
to place perfumes, smelling salts, dentifrices, elixirs, etc., etc. Beside the
bowl, place a soap dish, a box for
brushes, etc., etc.

The other smaller dressing table is
surmounted by an adjustable mirror,
framed in silk and muslin. The dec-
orations are like the larger. The
hair is dressed before this table. It is
supplied with all needful accessories,
beautiful brushes and combs marked
with the crest of their owner, delicate
perfumes, creams and lotions, powder
boxes, powder puffs, manicure set,
etc., etc. Projecting brackets for lights
should be on each side of this table.

The fireplace should be at the end
of the room, facing the windows. On
it place a porcelain clock and one or
two vases of fresh flowers. At one side

of the fireplace is a couch in blue or some other light color, brocaded with white, and here and there an ottoman and easy-chairs covered in subdued tints.

On either side of the small toilet table place a wardrobe. One of them must have three mirrored doors. The wardrobe is no longer used in artistic bed-rooms. It is within these doors (the two side ones open so as to enclose the beholder) that the effects of the hair dressing and toilet are reflected at every angle. The other wardrobe may be of lacquered wood without mirrors, and decorated with paintings of flowers. In this keep the supplies of bran, starch, powder, pastes, soaps, etc., etc.

Jugs and pails as well as bathgowns must be invisible. If there is no bath room attached to the dressing room, the tub—which we will speak of later—is brought into this room for the daily sponge bath, in lieu of that fuller bath which we are compelled to seek outside, or which sanitary reasons may forbid as a daily indulgence.

A More Simple Dressing Room.

The dressing room may be far more simple. One can expel from it all luxury, but a woman of taste will nevertheless succeed in making of it a charming little sanctuary, full of beauty.

Select a tasteful wall paper. Cover the floor with a rug. Drape the pine tables with a valance of cretonne bordered with a ruffle. Spread over the table a linen scarf trimmed with inexpensive lace, and on the table place bits of faience. Above it hang small

brackets covered like the table, on
which place the boxes, bottles, jewel
cases, etc., which may be graceful and
elegant despite their small cost. If the
mirror is ordinary, conceal the frame
by a drapery to correspond with the
table. This is easily arranged by
means of hidden tacks. Secure a
very simple wardrobe, which you can
greatly improve by painting and var-
nishing. Conceal the water jugs and
pails under the valance of the table.

If you are obliged to keep your
apparel in your dressing room you
should have a few shelves at the end
of the room on which to place the
boxes, bundles, etc., and beneath them
a few hooks from which to suspend
garments. All this should be concealed
behind curtains in harmony with the
drapery of the dressing table, not too

close to the wall, and so exposing the outline of the objects which it pretends to conceal, but hanging from the ceiling and projecting like an alcove. Under this drapery the zinc tub, which is not generally kept in view, may be hidden. Whenever it is possible, the dressing room should be large enough to move about in comfortably.

THE BATH ROOM.

ITS ARRANGEMENT AND APPOINTMENTS.

" Fresh from her bath
A rosy vision she."

THE furnishing of the bath room depends largely upon the means and
tastes of its owner. The millionaires
of New York have bath rooms which
rival those of the Roman Empresses.
In Europe, a few very rich women,
actresses, etc., spend a great deal on
the luxurious appointment of the bath
room. The walls are of onyx, framed
in brass moldings burnished daily.
From the ceilings are suspended
unique lanterns of rose-colored or
irridescent crystal. Behind a rich Oriental drapery, hung on gilded rings, is

concealed, when so desired, the rose-tinted marble bathtub. At the opposite end of the room, facing the tub, is a couch, covered by a white bear skin, on which, robed in an elegant dressing gown, the bather rests after the fatigues of the bath.

In one corner, also usually concealed by a rich silken curtain, are placed the shower baths, from which descend gentle or heavy showers on the satin skin of the divinity of this sanctuary. In the opposite corner is the porcelain tub for the sponge bath. The interior of this tub is painted in natural colors with water lilies, roses, and arums.

Besides the tub and bath are various conveniences, the faucets for hot, warm, and cold water, etc. The small utensils and accessories indispensable to the bath are placed on convenient marble shelves.

Utensils and Accessories.

When the bath room serves also as a dressing room it must have a dressing table, on which is placed a large porcelain, china, or silver ewer and basin, and all the smaller articles should be in keeping. There must be a smaller dressing table at which the hair is dressed. The movable mirror which is hung above it must be framed in natural flowers, renewed daily. The combs, toilet bottles, small jars, etc., and the powder boxes must be artistic *chefs-d'œuvre* made of precious substances, ivory, tortoise shell, silver, etc.

I had almost omitted to mention in its proper place the Dauphine bath, suitable for partial baths, and to enumerate the ottomans and low chairs covered with stuffs which are pleasant to the eye and soft to the touch, scattered here and there.

One word also concerning the large wardrobe with its three mirror doors, in which is kept the bath linen, the bath gloves, the straps, in a word, all the usual paraphernalia, creams, patches, lotions, etc., which for obvious reasons must be concealed from every eye.

There should not be in this luxurious bath room a single gewgaw, or a gown, piece of lace, or bit of jewelry. The clothes are kept in closets, and the jewelry and precious articles in one's bedroom.

But you will say that a bath room which is used in turn by all the mem-

bers of the family cannot serve at the
same time as a dressing room, and
besides we are not living in the land
of dollars, nor among the fashion-
ables.

With the above suggestions it would
be very easy to furnish a simple bath
room, from which are banished all
these unattainable elegancies, while at
the same time preserving comfort.
But we will add another description.

Have the walls of this simpler bath
room painted in oils (an imitation of
marble if possible). Over the tile or
wooden floor spread a carpet of lino-
leum. Ornament the ground glass
windows in the center with the mono-
gram of the head of the house.

Place in suitable positions the various tubs. Of course the large bath-
tubs will be placed under the faucets,

from which the hot and cold water pour into them, and near the drain through which the tubs are emptied. In front of these tubs is placed an india rubber mat, on which to step on leaving the bath. Within reach of the hand, that one may be able to secure the necessary articles while in the water, place shelves fastened to the wall for soap, sponges, etc. In many dressing rooms where the bath water is heated, the heater is provided with a drawer for linen, for it is necessary to use warm towels and to put on warm clothes on leaving the bath. These heaters can also be used to warm the dressing room.

The wardrobe contains the bathing linen, towels, sponges, dressing sacks, etc. On the little shelves place also soap, boxes of starch, jars filled with

bran, almond paste, perfumes, carbonate of soda (crystal), etc., etc.

On one corner place an alcohol
lamp used in preparing aromatics for
sudorific baths, which are sometimes
required in case of illness. There
are also portable heating machines for
preparing the vapor douche, both dry
and moist, and for moist vapor baths.
These accessories, and the shower
bath, the force pump for the douche,
shower, etc., are usually concealed
behind a portière.

Lastly, there should be a divan on
which to repose after the bath, a small
table in case one desires to take a cup
of hot, weak tea, a few seats, and a
sufficient number of racks on which to
spread the dry and damp linen. A
dressing table in this room would
be useless. One can be more comfort-

able in one's own dressing room or bed chamber.

Daily Baths.

A daily bath should be part of the moral laws of every class of society. If it is an impossibility to plunge daily into a bathtub, or if the doctor forbids a plunge bath, the sponge bath will prove sufficient for all purposes of cleanliness or health.

The human skin is a complicated net, whose meshes must be kept open and unclogged, in order that through them the body may throw off its impure secretions, which must be gotten rid of under penalty of pain and suffering, and sometimes death.

The healthy action of the skin is stimulated by the opening of the pores in the bath, especially if it is followed by friction with a brush or rough towel, etc. (Massage can be dispensed with if the touch of a strange hand is objectionable.) Many fevers and contagious diseases might be avoided by these means.

In cases of internal inflammation, bilious colic, congestion, there is no surer remedy than the hot bath. This bath has also effected most astonishing cures of obstinate constipation. When a person has been exposed to a contagious disease he should immediately take a hot bath. There is always a possibility that the disease will pass out through the pores of the skin. It should be remembered that it is very important to cool off gradually. Cleanliness of the skin has a decided influence on the assimilation of food by the body. It is known that well opened pores make a far finer skin than uncleanly people can boast.

But I shall be accused of writing a medical treatise. I merely wish to show that the healthy expulsion which the body performs through the pores teaches us the necessity of keeping them open and perfectly clean ; the least impurity, the finest dust, being sufficient to obstruct these little openings which were provided by wise Nature.

Think of the unfortunates of the Middle Ages, ignorant of the blessings of the bath ! "One thousand years without baths !" exclaims Michelet in one of his histories. Think of the pestilences, the hideous diseases which at that time scourged poor humanity ! In the time of Henry IV. the habit of bathing was still rare, for it is recorded of one of the great men

of the day that he asked why the
hands should be washed and *not* the
feet. How horrible!

If we knew the personal uncleanliness of the beautiful women of to-day
at the court of King Sun, we should
involuntarily shudder with disgust.

However, the famous coquettes in
all times have recognized the advan-
tages of the bath and ablutions. Isabeau of Bavaria, to whom some learned
man had mentioned the fact that Poppæa, Nero's wife, had her porphyry bath
filled with asses' milk, or the juice of
strawberries, was not behind her in
experiments of this nature. It was
thought that chickweed was refreshing
to the skin (which is perfectly true),
and the unfortunate wife of Charles
VI. bathed in strong decoctions of this
plant,

Anne Boleyn also took baths. You are doubtless familiar with the degrading sycophancy of the English noblemen who filled their glasses from her bath while she was in it, and drank to her health, with revolting jests.

Diana of Poitiers plunged daily into a bath of rain water.

In the eighteenth century, the ladies of the nobility wanted milk baths, like Poppæa, or chickweed, like Isabeau ; of almond paste, of flesh water (in which veal had been boiled), of the tears of the vine, of " distilled honey of the rose," of melon juice, of the milky juice of green barley, of flaxseed, to which was added the balsam of Mecca rendered soluble by the yolk of an egg. These were undeniably good for the skin ; but cleanliness does not require all these accessories.

A small bathtub invented for the use of the Dauphiness (Marie Antoinette) still bears her name. It is a round-bottomed basin, supported by a framework of wood and mounted on feet, the continuation of the woodwork forming an ornamental upholstered back. (In our day this is usually made of zinc.) For her full baths the princess had a decoction of wild thyme and marjory prepared, to which was added sea salt. The formula of this bath was made by Fagon, the chief physician of Louis XIV., who ordered these baths to be taken cold in winter and warm in summer, to bring the temperature of the skin into harmony with the atmosphere.

Marie Czétwertynoska, the mistress of Alexander I. of Russia, would only bathe in Malaga wine. This wine was afterward bottled and sold to people who were not ignorant of the purpose it had served.

Cold, Hot, and Sponge Baths.

Some people take a cold water plunge daily. One must be very healthy to stand such a bath, and I would advise no one to indulge in it until a physician has been consulted. Even when the cold bath has been prescribed, it is well merely to plunge in and get out immediately. The water should be from 50° to 59° Fahrenheit. Friction is indispensable after these baths.

The full hot bath is beneficial to those who have a tendency to vertigo. Its temperature should not exceed 92°. The tepid bath is the most in use. The water may be

heated to suit any taste from 68°
to 96°.

It is a mistake to prolong this bath.
One should not remain in it longer
than from fifteen to thirty minutes unless otherwise ordered by the physician.

When the full bath is unattainable
the sponge bath answers all the re-
quirements of cleanliness. The pores
of the skin are opened and cleansed,
which takes but a few moments. Instead of the bathtub and all its accessories, one needs only a large zinc tub,
a pail, and a small basin of water.
First pour the water over the chest,
then over the back, by squeezing the
sponge, which has been well soaked
in the basin. In this way each part of
the body is cleansed except the neck
and ears, which require more minute

attention and the finest of sponges and towels. Then we proceed to the more complicated cleansing of the hands, which demand other treatment. Dry with warm Russian towels.

In the sponge bath first use warm water, then, if one is in good health, lower the temperature of the water until, finally, the bath can be taken cold. In all cases the temperature of the room must be moderately warm. People whose lungs are weak should always bathe in warm water.

Of massage and friction we will speak later on. When one has been well rubbed after the bath, a quick walk in the fresh air is very advantageous.

Partial baths, of any kind, are almost always taken warm. It is unwise to bathe immediately after eating, as it seriously interferes with digestion. There should be at least three or four hours between a full repast and a bath.

The soap used for the bath must be perfectly pure and very slightly perfumed, if at all.

It is contrary to the rules of refinement or hygiene to bathe in water which has already done service for others, however healthy they may be. Mothers who take their children into the bath with them are doubtless ignorant of the fact that this is most injurious to these little creatures, whose delicate skins may absorb the effluvia, which are always unwholesome and often dangerous.*

---

* I have translated these pages literally, as their own best commentary on a condition of things for which we could find no parallel in the United States. It must be recollected that these are the words of a French noble-

Soothing and Refreshing Baths.

I shall not refer to Russian baths,
or Turkish baths, or even to vapor
baths. The last belong to the province
of physicians, who alone are fitted to
prescribe them ; the others require surroundings which it is impossible to
secure in a home.

But there are some baths within the

woman accustomed to every luxury. I question if a well-
to-do mechanic in America would consent to live and rear
his children where a bath would mean a half hour or more
passed " near the drain through which the tubs are emptied,"
and I should consider her a courageous woman who would
venture to suggest to the lowliest of our countrywomen that
" It is contrary to the rules of refinement or hygiene to
bathe in water which has already done service for others,
however healthy they may be. Mothers who take their
children into the bath with them are doubtless ignorant of
the fact that this is most injurious to these little creatures,"
etc. The American might not have the vaguest idea of the
definition of the word hygiene, but she would be certain to
experience a feeling of disgust at the suggestion in the first
part of this undoubtedly well-meant advice, and her sense
of decency alone would prevent her from permitting her
children to share her bath.—H. H. A.

reach of home hygienics which can be recommended with a clear conscience.*

In the springtime, when one is more susceptible to cold than at any other season of the year, it is best to bathe at night, just before going to bed, in order that the skin may profit by the warm moisture which it retains for several hours after leaving the bath. A delicious bath for this season is prepared from the barren strawberry plant or wild cowslip. Three handfuls of these perfectly fresh flowers are thrown into the bath, which is rendered odorous and soothing through the potency of their pale golden corollas.

The strawberry and raspberry bath into which Mme. Tallien plunged every morning (according to the gossips of the day) is prepared in the following

* The electric bath, if given by a trained expert, is refreshing, invigorating and soothing.—H. H. A.

manner : Twenty pounds of strawberries, two of raspberries; the fruit is
crushed and thrown into the bathtub.
The body emerges fresh and perfumed,
with skin soft as velvet, and tinted a
pale rose color.

The bath of lilacs, which is equally
odorous, is very calming to an overex-
cited nervous system.

A strong concoction of spinach also
makes an excellent bath ; but a recipe
just as good for making the skin fresh
and delicate is the following : sixty
grammes of glycerine, one hundred
grammes of rose water, diluted in two
quarts of water and poured into the
bath five minutes before using.

Some women dissolve almond paste
in their bath and perfume it with violet. Others prefer oatmeal and orange
flowers. Others use also benzoin bath

liquid, which imparts a milky appearance to the water.

The bran bath softens and refreshes
the skin. For this bath put two
pounds of bran into the tub with a
small quantity of water, three hours
before the bath. Of course the bran
must be contained in a small linen
sack.*

A bath of aromatic salts may be prepared without much expense. Crush
into powder some carbonate of soda
and sprinkle it with aromatic essences;
only a small quantity of these ingredients is necessary. This may be prepared at home. Then take essence of
fine lavender, 15 grammes; essence of
rosemary, 10 grammes; essence of eu-

---

* Bran and almond-meal bags, ready for immediate use,
may now be obtained in America. They are far superior
to the bran alone, and considered indispensable for the *bain
de luxe.*—II. II. A.

calyptus, 5 grammes; carbonate of
soda (crystallized), 600 grammes. Powder the crystals, add the essences,
mix together. Keep the bottles well
corked. For a full bath 315 grammes
of this compound will be required.
For toilet purposes one coffeespoonful of the mixture to a quart of
water.

An aromatic bath is invaluable as a
tonic. Take 500 grammes of wild
thyme and marjory and three quarts of
boiling water. Steep one hour, strain
and pour into the bath.

A bath both strengthening and delicious is made thus: Dissolve half
a pound of crystallized carbonate of
soda in the bath water, pour in two
handfuls of powdered starch, add one
coffeespoonful of essence of rosemary.
The temperature of the bath should

be from 96° to 98°.* Do not remain in longer than twenty minutes.

When the nervous system is exhausted, the following will renew its vigor somewhat: one ounce of ammonia in a pail of water.† The flesh will become as firm and smooth as marble.

I will not conclude this chapter without a suggestion for the benefit of rheumatic persons which will mitigate their sufferings. Make an emulsion of 200 grammes of soft soap and 120 grammes of spirits of turpentine; stir until the mixture forms a heavy suds. For one bath take half of this mixture, which has a most agreeable odor of pine. After remaining five minutes in the hot water, perfumed by the ad-

* This will make a very strong soda bath, and in many cases will leave the skin unpleasantly dry.—H. H. A.

† In my opinion an ounce of ammonia is sufficient for a full bath. It will not always have the effects here described.—H. H. A.

dition of the emulsion, one is sensible of a marked relief from pain, and a healthy glow is imparted to the whole body. At the end of a quarter of an hour a pricking sensation is felt, which is not at all disagreeable. Sleep follows immediately on retiring, and there is a marked improvement on awaking.

Massage and Friction.

The word massage is derived from a Greek word, *Masso*, I knead.

The *masseur* or *masseuse* kneads with the hand every muscular part of the body, exercises a traction on the joints in order to make them supple, and excites the vitality of the skin.

This practice comes from the East. Massage was known to the ancients, and the Romans practiced it. In the Russian massage, the hand of the masseuse is covered with a well-soaped glove. Sometimes the massage is followed by a light flagellation of birch switches.

Massage should follow the bath and not precede it. The skin, moistened by the water or vapor, becomes more supple or flexible, and is more easily kneaded. The patient is greatly fatigued when she leaves the hands of the masseuse, but this feeling is soon followed by a sensation of rest and comfort. It is dangerous to resort too frequently to massage; any excess will be followed by weakness instead of renewed strength. I have seen the good effects of massage in more than one form of disease, and in various climates. But in France a healthy woman would be unwilling to submit to it, even though that country had well trained masseuses, which is not the case.*

Fortunately, ordinary friction can replace this practice without assistance, thanks to the various appliances for the purpose of rubbing one's self over the shoulders and back, where the hands cannot reach easily. The friction is produced either with the bare hand, or by means of gloves or bands of horse hair, or of rough woolen or linen cloth. When no liquid is employed such friction is called dry.

* Facial massage, which has fallen largely into the hands of charlatans, is dangerous if abused, and the practice of frequently steaming the face cannot be too strongly condemned. In Paris, where the hygienic treatment originated, the face is never steamed oftener than once a month. A celebrated singer, anxious to retain the roundness and beauty of her throat, employed a masseuse *daily*. This excess of zeal resulted in almost total paralysis of the vocal chords.—H. II. A.

If you do not employ a masseuse, rub
yourself vigorously after the full or
sponge bath.   For the back and loins
hold the band in both hands and keep
it moving rapidly.   This mode of friction I recommend highly because it
can be accomplished without assistance.
It increases the strength, the vigor,
improves the health and, consequently,
the beauty.   After dry friction the
body may be rubbed with a piece of
flannel saturated in Russian aromatic
vinegar or in alcohol.

I could write a very learned chapter
on friction, under the dictation of one
of my friends, but I am not a physician,
and merely desire to give a few hygienic
suggestions.   It will be easy to procure
a treatise on this subject from the pen
of Dr. Gustave Monod, written with
the clearness and good nature which

are the distinguishing traits of this great surgeon, a man who marks each day by some noble action.

Sea baths. River baths.

A sea bath should not be taken on the day one arrives at a seaside resort. The diet needs to be modified, and all wine, coffee, and spirituous liquors should be abstained from, and the system allowed to become accustomed to salt air. The time selected should be when the tide is still. At low tide and at high tide, there are objections which it would take too much time to explain. It is unwise to take an ocean bath within three hours after eating.

It is dangerous also to bathe when excited; when suffering from acute or chronic disease, after a sleepless night, or after violent exercise. One should neither walk hurriedly to the beach nor bathe immediately after sleeping. Undress leisurely, and when the bathing costume is on walk up and down the sands in order to avoid the shock of a sudden plunge into the ocean.

It would be well for delicate women and children to take off their shoes and stockings a little time before going into the water, to warm their feet on the sand ; for people with poor circulation a glass of wine is recommended.

It is ruinous to a woman's hair to wet it, and no longer deemed necessary. Remain in the water only a few moments unless unusually vigorous. On leaving the water walk slowly to the bath house and rub yourself dry. Dress leisurely, and if the hair is wet dry it immediately, allowing it to remain unconfined for half an hour. Exercise in the open air is necessary after this bath.

As for infants, it is extremely dangerous to give them a sea bath before they are at least two years old. Even at this age, if they fear the waves, they should not be taken in. Young children lack the vitality to react vigorously, and without this, immersion is injurious. No child should be forced to endure the shock of the waves which it fears, since it is unwholesome to bathe while under the influence of violent emotions, and there is none stronger than fear.

Give the child its bath in a tub of salt water. Then allow it to run on the sand and pebbles, and wet its feet in the holes where the retreating waves have left their waters. It will thus take a sun and salt air bath.

In this way it will become accustomed
gradually to the sound of the waves,
their strength and violence, and be attracted toward them.   It will dream of
being cradled on them as on its mother's
breast.   Soon it will rush into the waves
and laugh at their rude caresses.

River bathing has many attractions
for the young and strong, and is very
strengthening to feeble persons who
take it under favorable circumstances.
It should not be prolonged, even when
one is strong and healthy, for fatigue brings on cramps and danger.
Neither should one indulge in this
sport, for it is a sport, without under-
standing the current of the water.
One unused to river bathing should
ask advice from those accustomed
to it.

The river bath requires all the pre-

cautions mentioned in regard to sea
baths. After a storm one should re-
frain from this bath, as the water becomes muddy. It should be avoided
also on rainy and cool days during the
summer.

*Hydropathy and Hydropathic Appli-
ances.*

We will first consider the derivation
of this word, which comes from the
Greek (not that I understand the language of Homer, but I have a wise
friend from whom I derive my Hel-
lenic information). Hydro means
water; pathy, cure or treatment.

Hydropathy is a mode of treatment
for diseases, especially in chronic cases,
exclusively through the use of cold
water, employed in the form of
douches, baths, ablutions, etc. It also

includes wrapping the patient, who is
stripped and placed in bed, in blankets,
and requiring him to drink abundantly
of cold water. Perspiration is induced,
and he is placed in a cold bath and
wrapped in damp sheets. However,
cold water should not be used inter-
nally or externally without the advice
of a physician, this treatment requiring
a practice and experience which is only
possessed by the medical profession.
Be it known, however, that the temperature of the water should not be
more than 48° nor less than 42° above
zero. The proper temperature is 48°.

It is not always easy to procure this
constant and invariable temperature
of 48°. It can always be found in
the Hydropathic Establishment of Divonne, in the Province of Ain, between
the eastern slope of the Jura and the

Lake of Geneva. Several springs
there unite, and their union forms a
torrent which is joined by the moun-
tain torrent. This body of water supplies with the health-giving properties
the pools which are devoted to the
different modes of treatment. It was
in this place that I studied hydropathy under all its forms, and received
all its benefits. After a few plunges
into the pools and the vigorous friction
which follows, one realizes a sensation
of comfort and warmth, an invigoration
throughout the whole body, the vitality
of which seems to have been renewed.

Water at 48° seems glacial to the
body which has a normal temperature
of 98°. When one plunges into the
pool it is hard to decide whether the
water is freezing cold or burning hot.
It feels as though one had been stung

by nettles. The immersion should not last over two minutes; on leaving the water the patient should be briskly rubbed until dry. (It reminds one of the rubbing down of a sweating horse.) If exercise is taken, or one is covered with blankets, a warm glow follows.

You need not fear taking cold from these sudden shocks by plunging into freezing water on leaving your warm bed while still moist from its heat. This is because the body has not had time to lose its natural heat; it receives a strong shock, and the skin is stung by the cold water as though pricked by pins. The cold is confined to the outer skin, and the blood soon returns to the surface. I assure you that you cannot take cold, and that hydropathy will cure a cold in its incipiency.

This ice-water treatment, which

seems hard to bear, and which frightens
you, becomes a pleasure, not only to
the more robust of humanity, but even
to the most delicate women, especially
if they can get the hydropathic treatment in their own homes. Many of
them are passionately fond of cold baths
and of douches, which are sometimes
administered in a stream, and again in
fine showers which cover the whole
body. The latter douche, administered
in a circle, is called the crinoline
douche. What memories are revived
by that name! Can you not see the
women of 1860 in their balloon
dresses? The crinoline douche greatly
pleases the more beautiful half of
humanity. "The circular douche is a
love of a douche, an elegant invention.
It is voluptuous; it is like a real dew
which caresses as softly as a bunch of

feathers;" thus an invalid of Divonne
enthusiastically expressed herself.

In fact, all the different methods of
administering cold water are delightful
to women in general, on account of
the benefit they receive, and because
their quivering nerves are toned and
soothed.

The maillot deserves also to be described. It is a pack. In one moment you are bandaged within the
folds of a wet sheet, under two
blankets, one of cotton, an eiderdown
coverlet, and still another covering.
All this is tightened, and fits closely to
the body. I defy you to move hand
or foot thus covered and strapped.
Soon you feel the return of warmth;
then you are thrown into the pool;
the effect is instantaneous, agreeable,
and soothing.

It is perfectly true that many chronic maladies, hitherto considered beyond remedy, have been cured by the practice of hydropathy. The fair sex has also derived benefit from all forms of this treatment. It is not to be denied that sudden changes of temperature, even the most violent, when followed by reaction, restore warmth to the surface, strengthen the functions of the skin, are a tonic to the muscles, relax the nerves; and feminine beauty profits by all these results.

I will not enumerate the diseases cured at Divonne, as we are only considering the subject from a certain point of view.

Of course the hydropathic cure will be more perfect, more satisfactory in the institution of which we have spoken, but at least in some respects it is possible to secure its benefits at home.

Baths, douches, showers, applications of cold water, friction, massage, all these are possible at home with certain surroundings. This is the reason why we have the necessary hydropathic appliances put in our bath rooms. The douche is taken by means of small force pumps through which we obtain, *ad hoc*, the water from reservoirs, under small or great pressure.

When the liquid column falls vertically, the douche is called descending; when it is directed horizontally, lateral; coming up from beneath, ascending.

In the first two mentioned, the reservoir is quite high and the tube large; the stream is, therefore, quick and powerful ; this constitutes the douche proper. In the latter, the reservoir is rather low and the tube small. The douche differs from the affusion ; the latter requires that the water should be applied by closer contact than by the douche.

Cleansing of Sponges.

There is nothing more repulsive than a greasy sponge, which looks, though it may not be, soiled. It inspires profound disgust. Soak such a sponge in milk for twelve hours. After this time rinse it in cold water and it will become new, minus, of course, the wear and tear. Lemon juice bleaches sponges admirably.

Sponges always become greasy and fishy, and then they are disgusting, despite cleansing with soap, which is not effectual. Chlorohydrate acid must be used, as it will remove the grease and bleach the sponge ; a single spoonful in a pint of water will be sufficient. Carbonate of soda may also be used for this purpose.

These are very minute details, but essential, which the mistress of the house should superintend herself ; servants often consider them too insignificant to receive attention.

PART SECOND.

PART SECOND.

GENERAL CARE OF THE BODY.

CLEANLINESS OF THE BODY.

" I will give out divers schedules of my beauty."

Confidential Hygienic Advice.

"CLEANLINESS is a half virtue," said Alexandre Dumas, "uncleanliness is a vice and a half." This is not severe enough; uncleanliness is an ugly vice, a low vice, and it has always been a surprise to me that women can be reproached with it, especially as it is incompatible with their desire to be beautiful and beloved.

During the darkness of the Middle Ages cleanliness was condemned as a remnant of ancient times (when the value of bathing was highly appreciated) and it was in the midnight darkness of those thousand years that this virtue was looked upon as a sacrilege.

It is, on the contrary, a sacrilege not to care for the body, which should be daily cleansed from the impurities imposed upon it by the conditions of physical life.

Even in this day, young girls leave school with limited ideas concerning cleanliness. Many mothers neglect to teach their daughters this part of hygiene, or to compel them to adopt the fastidious habits which they themselves have slowly acquired, not always without mortification.

Woman should keep her person with the most exquisite and refined cleanliness, that she may not fall short of man's ideal. Let mothers reject the stupid prudishness which influences them. A clean body is the necessary complement to a chaste nature, proper modesty, and refined habit. I knew an admirable mother, Danish by birth, English by education, French in her heart and by marriage. She was a pure woman with the highest sense of honor, and believed so thoroughly in the necessity of perfect cleanliness that she inculcated all its principles in her children. She. often said, "I have never been able to understand why it is not quite as important to keep the body clean as the soul or mind."

The Romans bathed their bodies before entering the Temple. Oriental religions require ablution before prayer. Does not this rule, which is hygienic as well as religious, prove that physical purity should accompany moral purity? The Koran constantly insists upon the necessity of frequent bathing.

While we are in so many respects superior to the Orientals, should we desire, on these all-important points, to remain far inferior to them?

Physicians, who are consulted by all classes, are forced to admit that we have progressed but little in cleanliness. We may justly ask why those who care for our bodies do not teach us that physical "half virtue" as the physicians of the soul teach us purity of spirit and mind. In ancient times they were inseparable; as proof of this

I will refer to that Normandy superstition which existed sixty years ago,
and perhaps still exists : as soon as a
person died a large basin of clear water
was prepared, " in order that the soul
might purify itself before taking its
flight." I see in this a symbol of
those ancient religions which com-
manded ablutions as a means of puri-
fication, concealing the hygienic law
under the theocratic.

Shall we in this period of brilliant
civilization continue to ignore the
most elementary rules of human dignity?

Animals, which do not possess our
hands with their opposing thumbs,
which have none of our means for securing cleanliness, clean their bodies,
lick their fur, or prune their feathers
through some hygienic instinct, and

yet man, their king by virtue of his reason and divine intelligence, neglects his body! Woman, that marvelous creation, will submit to having her satin skin, with its pearly tints, dishonored by impurities! No, no. The noble human body should be religiously cleansed each night and each morning from the stains and impurities which may attach to it, and which are the result of its being subjected to the material and animal laws under which it exists. Since we are not pure spirits, and must live as human beings, we are forced to submit to the conditions of our life, but we have it in our power to ameliorate them.

Believe me, cleanliness draws us nearer to the angels of light; uncleanliness, on the contrary, tends to draw us nearer our earthy origin. Cleanliness is indispensable to health and beauty.

To keep the pores of the skin open, one should bathe daily in cold or warm water; ill health and age are thus retarded. The result of uncleanliness is a flabby and unwholesome condition. The well cleansed skin is soft, smooth, fresh; a skin on which perspiration and dust have accumulated in layers becomes dry and feverish. But it may be said that it is not possible for the greater number of people to take a daily bath, as they lack the facilities and the time. The sponge bath— which is all sufficient for the purposes of cleanliness—requires only a few moments each day. Once or twice a week at least, one should take the time necessary for a full bath. This is the very least attention our bodies require.

It is not possible to fix the maximum of cleanliness, for there is no danger of our exceeding it. There are persons so scrupulously clean that they wash the esophagus, the stomach, and the intestines every morning, swallowing, for this purpose, a large glass of water, either hot or cold, according to the state of the health; others have recourse to Molière's instrument, solely as a means of securing cleanliness. We take it for granted that they are as careful to secure the cleanliness of the exterior of their bodies.

The least neglect of cleanliness is inexcusable. We wrong ourselves if we do not respect our bodies sufficiently to keep them vigorously clean and spotless. Nature soon punishes us for carelessness by sending disease and premature old age upon us.

Immersions and baths, with the aid of soap, lotions, etc., will render the body strong and flexible, and give it a power of resistance. Water has the virtue of dispelling fatigue and destroying the germs of disease. While cleansing the body it purifies our souls and gives us "A healthy mind in a healthy body."

THE FACE.

FACIAL ABLUTIONS.

" ' Tis not the eye, the lip, we beauty call,
But the joint force, and full result of all."

I<small>T</small> is well known that the pores of the skin should be kept open in order to perform thoroughly their functions, and that washing is an excellent means to relieve them of the secretions or accumulations which obstruct and close them.

Mme. Patti has been accused of never washing her face,* but this is contrary to all laws of hygiene. There are, however, precautions to be taken when washing the face. If there is

* There is, of course, no truth in this statement.— H. H. A.

any eruption on the face, warm water should be used. By this means the blood is driven away and the congestion relieved.

When it is very warm, or when the face is heated, do not wash in cold water. Bathe with warm water with pure soap. Take care to rinse thoroughly, so as to remove every particle of soap. Powder lightly, allowing the powder to dry on the face.

The face should be then carefully wiped on a piece of soft linen. Rough friction, with a coarse towel, has the effect of thickening some skins. It is well to remember that the skin requires the same delicate care that we bestow on fine porcelain or other rare treasures.

The face should never be washed in too much water; that is, water should not be dashed upon the face. Facial ablutions should not be too frequent, repeated several times in the course of a day.

I know one celebrated beauty who always washes her face with her own dainty hand. She then dries it on a soft piece of thin flannel. A flat facial sponge is better than the hand.

It is said that one of our society beauties every night on going to bed saturates a toilet towel in very hot water, wrings it, and applies it to her face, keeping it there for half an hour. This woman has no wrinkles.

A woman, fifty years old, whose skin is as smooth as that of a young girl, has never used anything on her face but hot water, which she believes prevents the skin from becoming flaccid and wrinkled. One of her friends does the same, but immediately after washes her face in cold water (Russian bath), and her sister uses hot water at night and cold in the morning.

All these apparent contradictions depend doubtless on different conditions of the skin. A well known physician advises washing the face in cold water in the winter, and in summer in warm or hot water, thus establishing harmony with the existing temperature. All of my relatives, who have fine complexions, bathe in cold water. Hard water, which does not dissolve the soap, should not be used for bathing, especially the face. If one cannot obtain either rain or river water, one should at least soften the hard water by using a little borax or a few drops of ammonia.

Alcoholic essences in the water in which the face is washed are very injurious.* Too frequent applications of alcohol to the skin dry and harden it, and prevent the performance of its functions and its consequent nourishment by the air and the humidity of the atmosphere.

On the other hand it is inadvisable to expose the face to the air immediately after washing it. Such exposure is apt to make the skin coarse and rough. Half an hour at least should elapse before going out. It is for this reason that women of leisure prefer to wash their faces at bed time.

It is necessary to use soap on the face. It should be carefully chosen— which subject will be considered later —not used too frequently, and never in very warm weather.

* A little scented water may be used without harm, and is a tonic for the skin.—H. H. A.

Lemon juice cleanses the skin very well, and sometimes serves the purpose better than soap. Strawberry juice has the same effect, besides being very improving to the skin.

A walk in the rain is more cleansing to the face than a Turkish bath. Wrapped in a hooded waterproof cloak, walk for an hour in the rain without an umbrella, allowing the face to be deluged by the heavy or fine showers. Not only the rain but the moisture in the atmosphere will dampen the tissues and wash them thoroughly, effacing from the skin those wrinkles produced by the artificial heat of the house, the results of a dry atmosphere. Tranquil, sufficient sleep and walking through the rain, it is said, were the only beauty philters employed by Diane de Poitiers, who walked each day, no matter what the weather, and never used an umbrella, for the very good reason that they had not yet revived that Roman custom.

Complexion. Color.

Caucasian women have always been and always will be interested in the purity, the freshness, and the brilliancy of their complexions. It is perfectly true that a fine color and a fair skin are great attractions, and no woman can ever be beautiful if her complexion is poor.

We often think that the color and texture of the skin may be improved by external means. This is, to some extent, a mistake. The complexion, whatever it may be, depends much on the health, the constitution, and the temperament. It is plain that we should look to hygiene rather than to cosmetics to supply the defects of color.

There are families in which a fine complexion is inherited. It may be taken for granted that the race is healthy, pure-blooded, has never been tainted by those horrible diseases which afflict humanity. A celebrated beauty was once asked the secret of the rose tint of her cheeks, the delicacy of her veined skin. "Healthy and virtuous ancestors," was her laconic reply.

A complexion which is too highly colored, especially if the color is deep and extends over nearly the whole surface, is neither desirable from an æsthetic nor from a hygienic standpoint. It indicates plethora. It will be noticed that those persons who are afflicted with high color, whose eyes even are veined in red, are usually large eaters, lovers of ease, and that they are averse to fatiguing exercises. In order to tone down their color, they should restrain the appetite, select less succulent food, take less ease, and discipline their bodies, for their blood is too rich. Their health will be improved by the directions here given; headaches, confusion of thought, dizziness, will disappear. From violent, the color will become merely brilliant, which is a very different thing, for even very bright color is not objectionable when it covers only the cheek as it makes the rest of the face fairer by contrast.

The hectic flush, which is only seen on the cheek-bone, is too often an indication of consumption. Unfortunately hygiene alone is not sufficient to remove the cause.

When the complexion is muddy, wan, pasty, too white, greenish, yellow, or purple, it is always a sign of bad health. A muddy skin is sometimes natural, but more frequently indicates dyspepsia, feeble circulation, etc.

A pale skin is usually due to a life spent within doors, lack of exercise, the habit or necessity of avoiding sunlight and daylight. A pasty skin is the result of a lymphatic temperament. An olive skin does not always indicate disease; it may have been inherited from some creole ancestor. A too white skin, without proper admixture of color, shows a person in serious ill health, although sometimes there are no other indications. A purplish complexion may come from some affection of the heart. A yellow skin requires especial attention. It is plain that care and precaution should be taken when the complexion is defective.

Hygiene is in many cases sufficient, and we will try to trace the prominent outlines of this preventive treatment, at least so far as women are concerned.

A thin woman may enjoy good health but never has a fine complexion, according to the proverb " there is no fine skin on bones." Later on we will show how to gain flesh, and explain how necessary it is to repress impatience and irritation, which dry up the blood more surely than illness or even grief. Intense artificial heat is also very destructive to the skin.

Cold is unfavorable to brunettes, warm air to blondes. Wind makes the face bluish or pale. Avoid walk-

ing against the wind.   The abuse of
the habit of kissing is injurious to the
complexion.   There are many parents
who object to their children being
kissed frequently, because it injures the
skin of the child.

Later we will give the proper diet
for a good skin and its preservation.

Wrinkles.

Wrinkles are often the result of bad
habits, such as a repeated drawing of
the eyebrows which forms small lines
between the brows. Lifting the eyebrows uselessly results in long trans-
verse lines on the forehead, and adds
at least five years to the real age. An
artificial, stereotyped smile imprints
two heavy furrows from the nose to
the corners of the mouth. Novel

reading far into the night often results
in the crows-feet which disfigure many
pretty faces.

Those who laugh much have little
lines at the base of the cheeks near
the mouth, but these are not objectionable. It is only necessary to take
note of those that are produced by
causes which may be easily overcome.
Gayety is a virtue which should not be
suppressed. Suffering traces wrinkles
on worn faces, but they disappear on
the return of health.

To retard the appearance of wrinkles
and lessen the fullness around the chin,
wash and dry the face from the top
downward; to avoid crows-feet, wash
the eyes from the temples toward the
nose. It is a mistake to fill up the
hollows between wrinkles with rice

powder.   It only serves to bring them
out in relief.*

Some rich women, whose complexions have been injured by overheated
houses, spray their faces with fresh
water fifteen minutes before going to
bed.   This effaces wrinkles and moist-
ens the skin.   Vases filled with water
will evaporate in air and neutralize the
painful effects of a dry, burning heat.
Wet cloths, frequently applied, produce still better results.

The fear of wrinkles induces many
women to submit to painful processes
in the hope of driving away these pre-
cursors of old age.

This is the method employed by a
society woman for effacing the wrinkles
which are produced by late hours and

* By proper treatment, by which I do not mean facial
massage as it is now generally practiced in New York,
wrinkles may be not only retarded but removed.—H. H. A.

dissipation. If she is annoyed she goes to her bed and remains until her fatigue has passed away or her vexation has vanished and her good humor is restored. She arises refreshed, beautiful, and amiable, her face devoid of wrinkles. She declares that if all women will follow her advice in similar circumstances, they will prolong their youth, calm their nerves, and acquire a desirable evenness of temper. A *débutante*, who was as fresh at the close of the season as at the beginning,. kept her beauty by remaining in bed all day Sunday. When summer came she was the only one of the family who did not seem to require a change of air.

Lady Londonderry, an English beauty, retains her youthful charms, which defy the ravages of time, at the cost of infinite pains. Every tenth

day she spends in bed sleeping until
she awakens naturally, then takes a
warm bath, returns to her bed, where
a light breakfast is served, tries to
sleep again, and if she does not succeed remains quietly there doing nothing, almost without thinking, in her
darkened room. At six in the evening
she arises, dines in her dressing room,
and remains near the fire inactive until
ten o'clock, when she returns to her
bed. This programme she never alters,
and I must confess that it agrees with
her marvelously. Occasionally her
maid reads to her a light, unexciting
romance.

If happiness depended upon worldly
success and the preservation of physical beauty, this method would doubtless be more reasonable than a resort
to artificial aids to repair the traces of

years. But think of the selfishness of
a wife or mother who thus neglects
her most sacred duties.

Surely there can be no harm in taking care of nature's gifts. It is proper
to preserve the hair and keep it beautiful, to keep the teeth white and even,
the complexion fresh and pure, etc., etc.
But there is a limit to everything. A
certain amount of coquetry should be
encouraged, but when it goes beyond
reasonable bounds, and causes neglect
of the duties of life, it is unpardonable.
Old age will come, and our children
prefer a tender, serious, and devoted
mother, with a slightly tired face, to
a frivolous and an indifferent one,
though she be still beautiful.

If a woman has no children, and life
is devoid of the boundless joys of maternity, she would do better to spend

her time in cultivating her mind. Once more I urge all women to believe that the moral nature is as worthy of attention as the physical. It is better to have an added wrinkle with each new virtue, than a smooth brow and the faults of a child.

However, if it is a possible thing, I would advise perfect repose of the face for a moment five or six times each day. The eyes should be closed, the muscles relaxed, and the face kept perfectly placid. These little halts in the occupations and anxieties of life retard greatly the traces which time imprints upon our faces.

Sunburn.

When from exposure to the hot sun or wind your fair skin has been sunburned, my dear friend, you are justly

distressed. However, it is an easy matter to restore to your complexion the
dazzling fairness of which you were
rightly proud.

Bathe your face at night with an
infusion (cold) of fresh cucumbers
sliced in milk. A decoction of tansy
in buttermilk is still more efficacious.
Buttermilk alone is excellent.

Another means of overcoming the
effects of sea or wind is to wash the
face with the juice of green grapes
prepared in the following manner:
Wet the grapes and powder lightly
with alum; wrap in a white paper
and cook under hot ashes. When
the grapes become tender they are
sufficiently cooked. Remove them
from their covering and squeeze into
a cup. Wash your face in the liquid three times within twenty-four

hours. This remedy is said to be infallible.

Many persons believe that the complexion grows dark if the face is washed at midday. " Midday, god of the summer, shining over the plain," should be feared by all delicate complexions.

If, as a foreign physician maintains, the electric light tans the skin as effectually as though the face had been exposed to sunlight, the moon might have the same effect. After all, it is said that she "eats into stone," why not into the skin? The Marechale d'Aumont, "as beautiful in her old age as in her youth," lived in mortal dread of the evening dew and the moon.

Let us return to the evil effects of the sun. The Italians resort to a very

simple method when they wish to
obliterate the injurious effects of salt
air and sunshine after a visit to their
villas, the shores of the Adriatic, the
Tyrrhenian Sea, or the lakes. They
bathe the face with the white of an
egg, well beaten, let it dry on the skin,
and rinse it off in soft water after
fifteen minutes. The treatment is repeated three or four times, and always
at night, just before retiring. This
last prescription, and that of drying the
face on a soft towel, are very important. The reasons were given under
the head of "baths."

Lastly, good results may be obtained
from the use of a mixture of lemon
juice and glycerine, equal parts. If
the skin will not stand glycerine—of
which we will speak later on—use rose
water instead.

Freckles.

Freckles are the despair of blondes, and even of brunettes with fair skins. Some physicians attribute freckles to too much iron in the blood. It has been proven that the abuse of iron tonics is often the cause of these yellow spots which disfigure more than one fair countenance.

Others say that freckles indicate a delicate constitution and feeble circulation.

By a few very simple precautions freckles may sometimes be prevented.

One of my friends used the following mixture with success: One part of tincture of iodine to three parts of glycerine, applied to the freckles before going to bed.

Another remedy is the following:

one-half pint of oil of turpentine; dissolve in it seven grammes of pulverized camphor; add two grammes of oil of sweet almonds.

The following is another excellent remedy: twenty-eight grammes of crushed camphor and 112 grammes of pure olive oil. Let the camphor dissolve slowly in the oil.

Applications of buttermilk are also excellent.

In some country, I do not now remember which, an odorous water for the complexion is made from the lily by heating it in a bain-marie;* a little salts of tartar is dissolved in this liquid.

The following remedies are also recommended: in twenty centigrammes of rose water dissolve sixteen centigrammes of borax.

* The Puritan Cooker is the best.—II. II. A.

Fresh beans, boiled in water, crushed and applied as a poultice on the freckles, will produce excellent effects.

Make a mixture of vinegar, lemon juice, alcohol, oil of lavender, oil of rose, oil of cedar, and distilled water. Apply to the freckles on retiring and wash the face in soft water next morning.

Two parts of sugar of water cress to one of honey is highly recommended for removing both large and small freckles. Strain through a cloth and apply morning and night.

Our ancestors, who were very careful of their complexions, wore in winter black velvet masks to guard the face from the effects of the cold, and in summer replaced them by masks of taffeta, to protect their delicate complexions from the "darts of Apollo," which bring

out these much dreaded spots. If we
cannot restore the fashion of masks in
springtime, when the buds begin to
blossom in the fields and freckles to disfigure the cheeks, we can wear a corn-
colored veil while walking. It would
be too tedious to explain on scientific
grounds how under this yellow veil you
will be as safe as under the old masks,
but I can answer for its efficacy. You
may reply that this color is not becoming. It is perhaps a question
whether you place more value on the
admiration of the world in general, or
the members of your own household.

When traveling, wash your face only
at night. Add to the water a few
drops of the benzoin bath liquid. Virginal milk is another name for this
mixture. Under no circumstances expose your face to the fresh air until it

has been well dried and lightly powdered.

Carrots are said to be a specific for the complexion, and are strongly recommended for freckles. In place of *café au lait*, breakfast off a thin porridge of carrots and a piece of dry bread.

Warts.

It was Montaigne, I believe, who said: "I love Paris, even its warts." This may be true of a large and superb city, but a beautiful or pretty face is terribly disfigured by the little hard, round tumors, commonly called warts. Therefore we give a few simple remedies which may destroy them without any risk.

No. 1. Administer small doses of sulphate of magnesia (Epsom salts). Dose for an adult from four to six grammes daily for a month. In most cases the warts will disappear at the end of two weeks.

No. 2. Formerly a plant was prescribed, called "Benvoire de Venus" (*Labrum veneris* or *virga pastoris* or *dipsacus fullonum*), on account of its leaves being in the form of a basin. The warts were rubbed with a reddish juice or water which was found in the hollow of the leaves.

No. 3. Some advise pressing the wart against the bone, rubbing it back and forth, until the roots become irritated and painful, and the wart drops off.

No. 4. Warts and wens are sometimes cured by rubbing them two or three times daily with an Irish potato. Cut off one end of the potato and rub the tumor with the pared surface. After each operation remove a slice of the potato.

No. 5. Rub the wart night and morning with the following salve : twelve centigrammes of chromate of potassia well mixed in fifteen grammes of soft animal fat or vaseline. The warts will usually disappear in the course of three or four weeks' treatment.

No. 6. Lemon juice will cause some warts to disappear. Touch them two or three times daily with a camel's-hair brush soaked in the juice.

No. 7. Take a slate and calcine it in the fire. Reduce it to powder and pour strong vinegar on the powder. You will thus obtain a liquid with which you can rub the excrescences. They will often succumb to this treatment.

No. 8. The heliotrope of Europe (the *verrucaria* of apothecaries) is highly esteemed. Its sugar, mixed with salt, causes warts and wens to fall off.

No. 9. Caustic, or nitrate of silver, also removes warts.* Touch them every two or three days.

No. 10. Some warts may be removed by soaking them several times each day in castor oil.

No. 11. Melt some essence of salt in water and bathe the warts in it. This caustic will dissolve them and cause them to peel off. This treatment requires great caution, especially if applied to the face.†

No. 12. Use also the caustic sugar of celandine.

---

* This should be applied only by a physician.—H. H. A.
† I cannot endorse this remedy.—H. H. A.

It is a mistake to suppose that warts are not sometimes contagious.

Skin Diseases of the Face.

One of my friends, who is a physician, has successfully treated herpes of the face by rubbing on the juice of a lemon.

Ringworms have been cured by bathing in the juice of strawberries. It is not easy to imagine a simpler or more agreeable remedy. It is certainly less repulsive than "rubbing the afflicted part with a live snail," which was formerly the custom. Strawberries are said to be a sovereign remedy for ulcers, and also for ringworms.

Strawberries used daily during the season will remove facial eruptions, pimples, etc.*

* Strawberry Cream is an excellent remedy for slight cutaneous eruptions ; but it is not a specific for all such evils.—H. H. A.

For eczema of the face, recourse should be had to poultices made of potato farina.

A decoction made of the fresh root of star-wort (fifteen grammes to one quart of water) is highly recommended. Take a pint of the decoction before eating, in two or three doses; the other pint at night, at least two hours after the last meal. The diet must be very strict—no wine, no coffee, no game, fish or pork of any kind. Strawberries, asparagus, cabbage, turnips, cheese (except Gruyère) are forbidden.

The same diet is prescribed for pimples. Besides this, use the following lotion and salve: Sublimate of sulphur thirty grammes; alcohol, twelve; distilled water, 200. Moisten a sponge in the mixture and wash the face. Re-

peat frequently. A medicated hot
vapor spray is sometimes excellent.
Salve : three grammes of oxide of zinc to
thirty grammes of vaseline. Mix thoroughly and use at night. The treatment should be interrupted twice during
the week for about twenty-four hours.
Wash the face in warm water before
applying the lotion.

The Duke of Edinburgh, son of the
Queen of England, is said to use onions
liberally in his diet for a skin disease.*

It is needless to say that these
simple remedies may be used for skin
diseases affecting other parts of the
body.

Depilatories.

There is another and more desperate
cause of annoyance among women.

* The value of the onion in such cases is well known.—
II. H. A.

I refer to the growth of hair which so often appears on the chin at middle age, and to the down which imparts a masculine appearance to the rosy lips of some young girls of twenty.

Do not despair. There are, fortunately, remedies for this affliction.

First. Removing these hairs with a small tweezer of steel is one of the common remedies. But the hair must be carefully pulled and not broken; it should be removed by a sudden jerk. Recently an operation by electricity to which the name of electrolysis* is given has been highly recommended.

Second. Make a wash of the leaves and roots of celandine distilled.

---

* Electrolysis is apt to leave scars; the hairs reappear unless the electric needle strikes the center of each hair follicle. This treatment is frequently unsuccessful and always most painful.—H. H. A.

Make a compress, apply to the hairy spot, allowing it to remain on all night. Continue until the hairs disappear.

Third. Sulphuret of soda, three grammes; quicklime,* ten grammes; starch, ten grammes. Add enough water to this mixture to make a paste, apply to the down, let it remain on for an hour, and then wash it off in soft water.

Fourth. Use polypode of oak; slit and cut into pieces, place in a cucurbite (vessel resembling a gourd used in distillation) and pour over it some white wine, which should cover the polypode a finger's width. Let it stand for twenty-four hours. Then distill in boiling water until no more evaporates. Apply in compresses on the afflicted

* This is a most dangerous ingredient. I cannot recommend its use excepting under a physician's advice.—H. H. A.

parts, keeping it on all night. Renew until the desired effect is obtained.

If it be true, as asserted, that lentils have the property of promoting the growth of hair, both in length and thickness, of producing mustaches, and of making beards heavier, women who have a tendency to hair on the lips and chin should rigorously abstain from indulging in this vegetable.*

Washes and Cosmetics for the Face.

Never use any kind of paint. All rouges injure the skin. Blanc de perle is dangerous.

It is said that the Chinese have discovered a harmless paint, made of beet juice, with which they color their cheeks.

* Some of the best and safest depilatories are made from formulæ which are secret and private property. They cannot therefore be given here.—H. H. A.

I give the recipes of a few excellent
washes, because I am certain they
are harmless, and some of them are
very refreshing to the skin. We
will begin with the most simple.

Greasy skins are benefited by washing in wine (the wines of France and
the Rhine) ; use about every fifteenth
day. If the complexion is dark, red
wine is preferable. The juice of fresh
cucumbers is still better for the skin.
Equally good is the water in which
spinach flowers have been boiled.
The juice of strawberries, of which we
have already spoken, is superior.

During the sixteenth century the
water in which beans had been boiled
was in vogue for the complexion.
This farinaceous water is entitled to
the fame which it possessed. Our
Gaulish ancestors, whose glowing

color was a subject of envy to the patrician Romans, washed their faces in the foam of beer. They also used chalk dissolved in vinegar. I scarcely know what to think of this solution, but I can assert that the foam of beer is still used with good results among the women of the North.

Belladonna (beautiful lady) derives its name from the use which the Italians of the Renaissance made of its juice to improve their complexions. "The Roman dames of antiquity, those great coquettes," says someone, I have forgotten whom, "esteem the hare's blood as the most precious cosmetic." This is certainly repulsive.

The following lotion is excellent: A wineglassful of lemon juice, a pint of rain water, five drops of essence of rose, well corked. Wash the face occasionally with this mixture, which often prevents the discoloration of the skin.

Soft and relaxed skins will be improved by the use of the following cosmetic (at intervals of eight days) : one part milk, one part whisky. Moisten a soft towel with the mixture, after having first washed the face. The results do not follow immediately, but within a year the skin will frequently contract, become firm, fine, and soft.

If you need emollients for a dry skin, put some fragrant oil into a jar of vaseline.*

The oil of cocoa enriches dry skins.

The Princess of Wales is said to use a mixture made of half a pint of milk and the juice from a slice of a Portu-

---

* It will, however, produce superfluous hair.—II. H. A.

guese lemon, which she applies on retiring, washing her face in soft, warm water next morning. As a matter of fact, she uses Recamier cream.

Lastly, here are veritable cosmetics :

Toward the end of May take a pound of the very freshest, purest butter. Place it in a white basin, and expose it to the sun, where it will be well protected from dust, etc. When the butter has melted, pour over it some plantain water, mix well by means of a wooden spatula, and let the sun absorb the water. Pour in more plantain water and repeat five or six times during the day. Continue until the butter has become as white as snow. The last few days add a little orange flower and rose water. Cover the face at night with this salve, and

carefully wipe off in the morning.
This is a good and old recipe of the
time of the beautiful Gabrielle.

Here is one that dates from the time
of the Crusades: Take out the yolks
of six hard boiled eggs, and replace by
myrrh and powdered candied sugar in
equal parts. Put the ends from which
the yolk has been taken together
again, then place the six eggs on a
plate before the fire. Mix the result-
ing liquor with thirty-two grammes of
fat pork. This mixture forms a pomatum, with which the face is covered in the morning. Let it dry and
then wipe it off carefully. This secret of beauty was, it is said, brought
from Palestine by a brave knight
beloved by the sultana. His lady-
love probably heard of his infidel-
ity, but she doubtless forgave it on

account of the cosmetic which he brought back from the harem.

Cosmetics for the Hands, Arms, etc.

The above recipes may be used for the neck, arms and hands. Here is still another to be used at night when the arms and shoulders are uncovered:

Glycerine, rose water, oxide of zinc. This preparation has the advantage of not whitening the coats of partners in a dance.

The Use of Rice Powder.

It is sometimes necessary to powder the face, and we have stated under what circumstances. But powder should be applied lightly and artistically in order to impart to the skin the velvety softness of the peach.

A face powdered like a clown's is

ridiculous, and as unbecoming as vulgar. Powder on the face should be imperceptible, and if used with discretion is not to be condemned.

Take up but a small quantity of powder on the puff, and pass lightly over the face. Care should be taken not to powder the eyebrows, and the lips must be carefully wiped to remove any powder which may have fallen. The whole face, except the eyes, the eye-brows, and lips, should receive a touch of powder.

HAIR.

DARK AND LIGHT.

Her fair soft hair
That like a golden shower about her fell.

WHO has not envied the "kingly mantle" sung by de Musset?

Truly, it is a magnificent decoration which nature has bestowed on a chosen few. We should know how to preserve it, no matter how poor may be our own.

The hair, to be truly beautiful, should be thick, long, fine, and lustrous. If your hair is thin, short, coarse, dull, do not despair of being able by intelligent effort to improve it.

All the qualities which we have enumerated are insufficient to some

women if their beautiful hair is as black
as the raven's wing. They prefer to
be blonde, like almost all the charming
or bewitching women whose names
have been preserved in history. Eve,
it is said, was as blonde as honey; the
hair of Venus rippled on her divine
shoulders in golden floods; the hair of
Ceres was corn color. The queenly
brow of beautiful Helen, whom the
Trojans so adored, was crowned with
hair as yellow as wheat. Salome,
who asked for and obtained the head
of St. John the Baptist, had yellow
hair. At least the old masters painted
her as they did every patrician maiden,
as a blonde. Lucretia Borgia, Lady
Macbeth, Mary Tudor, Bloody Mary,
were all blondes. Queen Elizabeth
had red hair. Catherine and Marie
de Medici were also blondes.

Cousin describes the hair of the Duchess de Longueville, whom he worshiped, in the following manner : " The finest of ashen blond hair falling in rich curls around the pure oval face, and spreading over the perfect shoulders." Anne of Austria, Madame de Sévigné, whose coiffure is still admired, the gentle La Vallière, were all blondes. The golden hair of Marie Antoinette and Mme. de Lamballe would alone have sufficed to make them beautiful.

Mme. Emile de Girardin had also beautiful light hair. One of the charms of the Empress Eugenie was her hair, which was golden red.

I admit that I have a preference for light hair, especially when golden or reddish. The Greeks, in the time of Pericles, washed their hair in lye water in order to bleach it, and afterward applied an oil made from the fat of goats, ashes of the beech tree, and certain yellow flowers. The hair was allowed to float on the shoulders until dry. The Germans were proud of their light hair. Those who did not have it by nature had recourse to art. Bathing the hair in beer was considered efficacious. So was a plaster of lime. The Roman ladies hated their dark hair, and Ovid tells us that they wore blonde wigs, for which high prices were paid in Germany. It is well known to what suffering the Venetians submitted in order to produce in the hair those bright bronze tints which are called by Titian's name.

In our day many women scientifically dye their hair a mahogany color. This is hideous. Others, who are already blonde, make their hair still lighter by the use of oxygenated water. The English wash their hair in rum, into which they put an infusion of bitter apples (colocynthis), to prevent the hair from growing darker with age.

It seems that in other days (those blessed other days!) there were many more blondes than in our time. Would you know why even in the North, the hair has a tendency to grow darker from one century to another? " Heaven," said a humorist, "sent upon the earth many women with golden hair, that they might charm the other half of humanity. Seeing this, the devil, who hates men, sent cooks. These, with their sauces and ragouts, disordered the human liver and produced the desired result — dark skin and hair."

Under this jest there may lurk a truth.

Arabian women and the feminine subjects of the Shah prefer dark hair. But they often tint their beautiful black hair with henna. The leaves of this plant, reduced to powder in water, make a cosmetic which is carefully rubbed into the hair. This paste is removed by washing the hair in indigo water a few hours afterward. It retains from this application a bright reddish color for several days.

The Russians admire chestnut colored hair above all other, and maintain that Christ had hair of this color. Auburn hair is much admired in England. It suits well the fresh faces of the daughters of Albion.

Hair Dressing.

After all, despite my own preference for blondes, I would advise no one to change the color of the hair, though it be as black as Erebus. Nature gives each face the framework most suitable to it. She never needs correction on that point.

Great care should be taken to dress the hair becomingly. It is curious to see how many women in arranging their hair disregard its color and texture. It is as useless to persist in crimping straight hair as to smooth or plaster down curly or waving hair, though it is admitted that certain types require the aureole which accompanies fluffy hair. Black hair is not improved by crimping; it requires bandeaux, long and lustrous curls, heavy tresses,

Auburn hair may be crimped, made fluffy, not plastered together, and its tints subdued. Heavy braids of chestnut hair are very handsome. Blonde hair admits of any style of dressing, and is alike charming in bandeaux or in a nimbus around the brow. Why not dress the hair to suit the face, no matter what is the prevailing fashion ?

Hair should be allowed to grow gray naturally. All dyes made of mercury or lead are dangerous, and destroy the beauty and color of the hair. Let us gracefully accept the snowy locks of age. They harmonize with the face which has been changed by time and sorrow. Many faces are softened and beautified by white hair. It is more graceful and dignified not to attempt to repair the ravages of time.

I am opposed to powdering even gray hair, as it makes the features appear hard. The delicate faces of the eighteenth century would have been still more charming if the Marechal de Richelieu had not conceived the idea of hiding his first silvery hairs under powder. Besides, as there is nothing new under the sun, the conqueror of Port Mahon has not even the merit of having discovered the use of hair powder. The ancient Greeks, who sometimes bleached their hair, were also accustomed to powder it a pale blue, the changeable colors of the dove's neck, or of honey from Hymettus.

Hair which is too tightly drawn or twisted and plastered is not becoming. It has the appearance of an effort to get rid of it, instead of embellishing it.

The effect of this is certainly disastrous. The hair should be dressed with freedom, which also conduces to its healthfulness.

Long and thickly crimped bangs are vulgar. A few short, light rings, above the brow, greatly soften the face. Hair dressed high on the head is not becoming to women past a certain age. Hair dressed low at the back of the neck is very graceful and youthful. Dress the hair according to the cast of features. A small, thin woman appears ridiculous with her head enlarged by the arrangement of the hair. If the forehead is high, full, the features large, the face is most unbecoming with hair dressed *à la Chinoise*. Parting the hair on the side produces a youthful effect, but is apt to make the most delicate face appear masculine. Avoid eccentric hair dressing : never increase the size of the head by a mass of false hair. The head has a greater refinement and distinction, if its shape is left unchanged and in harmony with the body which it crowns.

Aged women are greatly improved by covering the hair (even while it is still beautiful) with a bit of lace, which falls in graceful folds about the face. Light shadows of lace go far toward concealing the ravages of time.

Care of the Hair.

The fashion of crimping the hair with hot irons, etc., is destructive to its beauty. What shall we do with our bangs, which have grown coarse by frequent cutting, when fashion decrees an opposing mode ?

Many women to save their hair wear false fronts, a custom not without danger. Frequently false hair, though apparently clean, is a cause of contagion. Hair cut from the heads of the Chinese often spreads disease. Fortunately this hair is easily recognized, as it is always coarse, rough, black, and glossy.

False hair should be frequently renewed. Taken from a living head, it retains its vitality for about two years, sometimes even longer. Afterward it becomes uneven, stiff, matted, and can no longer be used. Hair cut from the dead is never used by hairdressers of good repute. Use as few pins as possible in fastening the hair, in order not to irritate the scalp, which may be scratched by them. It is well sometimes to change the style of dressing the hair, as it is apt to grow thin when always arranged in the same way.

When the hair is worn parted, be careful to make a new part each day in order to prevent it from spreading. It is advisable to clip the hair in the first quarter of each new moon, and at the end of a year the hair will have lost nothing in length. I cannot believe that the silent orb of night has any influence on the growth of hair, but there may be occult mysterious influences which science has not yet explained. It is a certain fact that hair clipped at each new moon grows thicker.

It is well to sleep from infancy with the head uncovered, as the hair thus retains its beauty longer. On retiring the hair should be raised high above the ears, without pulling, plaited loosely in a single braid, and tied with a silk or cotton ribbon. Avoid wearing starched nightcaps, as the starch is injurious to the hair. When old age approaches it may be well to wear nightcaps.

Brush the hair well, using a soft brush, on going to bed and in the morning. The best brushes are made with short bristles. If the hair is combed from the roots downward without being divided in several parts, much harm may be done to it. The hairs would certainly be broken off, become uneven, and could never be made to look cared for. It is an excellent thing to smooth the hair with the hand. In Turkey, the slave intrusted with the care of the tresses of the Sultana, caresses the hair, rolls it in her hands until it is supple, brilliant, and looks like silk. Use grease, oils, and pomade as seldom as possible.

The Roman dames believed that walnut rind improved the luxuriance of their hair.

Cleansing of Hair.

The frequent use of a fine comb is fatal to hair, especially when it is falling out. However, it is necessary to cleanse the hair and the downy scalp.

One of my friends who has beautiful, soft, waving, lustrous hair, cleanses it occasionally with a mineral water.

The Chinese, who have abundant, but coarse hair, use a mixture of honey and flour.

The following is an English recipe : A teacupful of salt to a quart of rain water. After twelve hours this brine

is ready for use. To one cupful of the
mixture add one cupful of hot rain water. Wash the hair and scalp, rub well,
rinse, and dry with a towel.

The Italians cleanse their long and
abundant hair with a decoction of this-
tle roots.

The Creoles of Cuba make a decoction of the leaves of rosemary.
This water, they maintain, cleanses,
strengthens, and softens the hair.

This also is excellent. Take fifty
grammes of the roots of soap-wood
boiled in a pint and a half of water.
Wash with the hot preparation, then dry
the hair and scalp with warm cloths.

The yolk of an egg cleans the head
thoroughly and causes the hair to grow.
Only the scalp should be rubbed with
the yolk, and the head rinsed in hot
water. The beaten white of eggs is

also recommended as a simple and efficacious preparation for cleansing the hair. Rub the scalp and rinse in hot water.

The following are more complicated lotions for those persons who disdain to use the simpler ones.

First, for cleansing the hair and scalp, also for headaches, and to prevent the falling out of hair : take half a pint of pure rectified spirits, dissolve in it half a gramme of sulphate of quinine and allow it to infuse two days in a hermetically sealed bottle. After this time has elapsed add a pint of old rum and fifty grammes of yellow Peruvian bark, powdered ; let it stand three days. Pour on the liquid ; wash the sediment in about two-fifths as much water. Mix the two liquids, strain through filtering paper.

Second. The following druggist's formula may be easily prepared : Sulphate of quinine, three grammes, dissolved in Rabel water ; opopponax, ten grammes ; triturate in enough alcohol, 96 per cent., to dissolve it ; add essence of patchouli, three drops, essence of violet, five grammes, essence of bouquet, five grammes. Increase to six quarts by adding enough alcohol at 40 per cent. Throw into the liquid seventy-five grammes of Florentine orris, pulverized. Let it stand eight days and then strain.

The custom of shampooing originated in England. Take one quart of cold or hot water into which is melted thirty grammes of carbonate of soda and fifteen grammes of soap, cut into small pieces. Add a few drops of perfume and thirty grammes of spirits of wine. After washing with this preparation, rinse the hair in warm water. Afterwards rub the hair and scalp until dry, with warm towels.

The hair should always be thoroughly and rapidly dried. After drying, let it hang loosely on the shoulders, for an hour or two if necessary.

Hair, especially gray, may be cleansed with powder. Afterward it should be carefully brushed. This is an excellent method, though it is difficult to remove the traces of powder from dark hair.

Diseases of the Hair.

Dandruff is not only very disagreeable, but produces baldness. Before resorting to medical treatment for this disease, which is sometimes obstinate, because it depends on a bad state of health, try one of the following simple remedies : First, melt sixty grammes of crystallized soda in a quart of water ; add thirty grammes of cologne water. Moisten the hairbrush in the liquid and pass it each day over the affected part.   Second, a physician recommends the application of lemon juice to the scalp.   Keep the juice as much as possible from the hair.   Third, take ten grammes of Panama wood ; boil in a pint of rain water.   Wash the affected parts with this decoction two or three times each week.

When the hair falls out without apparent cause, it is diseased.   This is the case when the ends split.   Sorrow causes the hair to fall out.   For this there is no remedy save time and forgetfulness, and happier days.

An animal is known to be unhealthy if its hair is not soft and shiny.   With all due respect, it is the same with men and women. If this be the case, examine into your health and try to discover the trouble. A good treatment for hair under these circumstances is to rub the scalp with soap and a mixture of castor oil, sweet almond, and tannin.

A young girl of fifteen suddenly lost her hair without any perceptible cause. She neglected to have it cut close to the head as should have been done, and the result was that it did not grow out again. A physician recommended shaving the head and washing it three times each week with the following preparation: One-half ounce of coloquintida in a pint of good Jamaica rum. After standing three days it was filtered and put into well corked bottles. Before applying it the hair was vigorously brushed. The remedy was most successful, and the coloquintida changed the color of the hair to a beautiful shade of gold.

Baldness.

Baldness is not so serious a matter to a man as to a woman, for he has the comfort of knowing that he has many companions in his misery.

But a bald woman is really to be pitied. It is impossible to accept such a misfortune with resignation; she must conceal it by every means in her power.

She is often compelled to resort to a wig, or to caps such as are worn by dowagers.

The growing tendency to baldness among women has been attributed to the use of hot irons for crimping; to

false hair; to overheating the scalp by
headdresses. My own opinion is that
baldness is due principally to the use
of dyes.

We no longer wait for gray hairs,
but vary the color of the hair to suit
our caprices, and quite frequently
the brunette of to-day may appear to-
morrow with golden or even red hair.
Those who have black hair sometimes
stain it mahogany color. Blondes
whose hair is growing darker lighten it
by the use of oxygenated water, which
removes the color. Many women will
resort to any means rather than
allow the hair to grow gray naturally.
Such practices are much to be condemned. Let us remain as we are,
content to grow old gracefully.

It is time to begin to remedy the
evil, if only for the sake of future gen-

erations. Simple modes of hairdress-
ing should be revived, without the
addition of false hair, or the use of
crimping irons. Care should be taken
to cover the head with silk and not
wool; no velvet should be used in a
headdress; and above all dyes should
be abandoned. The natural color of
the hair should be preserved, and
allowed to grow darker or become
white; even gray hair should not be
powdered. In this way the hair will
remain abundant and vigorous, even
to an advanced age, and there will be
enough of it to dress becomingly.

Is there anyone who would not
prefer thick bandeaux, even though
streaked with silver, to a bald head or
a wig?

A woman so unfortunate as to be
bald may invent pretty headdresses of

lace to conceal her affliction. Mothers should teach their daughters how to prevent baldness by taking proper care of their hair.

Remedies for Falling Hair.

The juice of a lemon applied to the scalp is said to be a remedy for the falling out of dark hair.

The following recipe has been used successfully: Wash the head each night, rubbing in carefully the following mixture: one teaspoonful of salt and one gramme and a half of quinine, added to a pint of brandy; mix well.

I have seen this remedy prepared and know its good results: steep three common onions in a quart of rum for twenty-four hours; after this remove the onions and apply the liquor to the scalp every second day. The slight odor of onions soon disappears.

The English medical journal, the *Lancet*, recommends the following pomatum : tincture of jaborandi, fifteen grammes ; lanoline, nine grammes ; glycerine, sixty grammes. Mix with a little soft soap, and apply to the scalp every night.

Good results have been also obtained by using walnut leaves steeped in water. Dip a small sponge into the liquid, and moisten the scalp each night. In the morning use the following prescription : perfumed soft animal fat, sixty grammes ; tannin, two grammes ; tincture benzoin, six grammes.

A man whose eyes were treated by injections of pilocarpine had a new growth of hair at the age of sixty.

After an illness it is unwise to shave
the head. The hair will not fall out if
cut at intervals of three weeks. Each
time a certain quantity must be cut,
proportionate to the whole length of
the hair; the last cutting should be
about to the lobe of the ear. False
hair should not be worn, as it sometimes causes total baldness. From
the day on which the hair is first
cut, the head must be rubbed with a
mixture of equal parts of rum and
castor oil.

Hot sage tea is also recommended,
provided the head is well dried with a
warm towel.

Pomades and Hair Oils.

Some people have such dry hair that
they are obliged to use pomades to
prevent it from breaking off.

A physician recommends the use of rectified oil of vaseline (liquid vaseline) perfumed to suit the taste.

Inferior pomatums cause or hasten the loss of hair. Therefore, unless you can procure the very best from a well-known manufacturer, prepare them yourself.

The grease and the oils which are used, to be preserved from growing rancid, must go through a suitable process. Put in a bain-marie 200 grammes of fat or marrow, with six grammes of powdered benzoin and six grammes of pulverized balm of tolu. Stir constantly with a wooden spatula. After two hours of hard boiling, strain through a bit of linen. Benzoic acid possesses, like vanilla, the quality of preventing the fat to which it is added from becoming rancid. Vase-

line does not become rancid. To make
the pomatum take ninety grammes
of this prepared grease, sixty grammes
of marrow, and thirty grammes of
sweet almond oil. Perfume these substances while still slightly liquified
(not entirely cold or congealed), with
essence of bergamot, two grammes,
and essence of violet, four grammes.

Some persons use water in place of
pomatum, but nothing could be more
injurious for the hair.

Cleansing of Combs and Brushes.

Nothing is better for cleansing
brushes than ammonia; it does not
soften the bristles, as soap and soda do.
Put a teaspoonful of ammonia into
a quart of water, and soak the bristles
in the solution (keeping the ivory,
bone, or varnished back out of the

water). The brush must then be rinsed in fresh water and dried in the air, but not in the sun.

Combs should never be washed. They may be cleansed by passing a coarse thread or card between the teeth. There is also a small brush which is used for cleaning combs.

The greatest cleanliness is necessary for all articles used for dressing the hair.

If you use ammonia in your bath, avoid wetting the hair except when necessary, because ammonia fades the hair.

THE MOUTH.

" I saw her coral lips to move,
   And with her breath she did perfume the air."

A SWEET breath has an important
influence on beauty and the preservation of the teeth. If it loses its purity,
one soon becomes an object to be
avoided. It is evident how important a fresh breath is, and we should
not neglect proper care in preserving
it. Sobriety, health, an avoidance of
those bulbous roots, onion and garlic,
clean and healthy teeth,—these are the
general conditions which enable us to
retain until old age or until death a
breath as sweet and fresh as that of a
child.

Diseases of the mouth and stomach, neglected teeth, tartar, the abuse of alcoholic spirits, rich dishes (highly spiced) seriously injure the breath. When the cause is to be attributed to the stomach, to suffering from toothache, or a sore mouth, the use of purgatives, mineral waters, chalk powders, magnesia, bi-carbonate of soda is recommended.

Bad teeth should be instantly removed. If a dentist cannot be reached immediately, recourse should be had to chewing small pieces of Florentine orris root, to prevent the unpleasant breath caused by bad teeth.

The Japanese eat the bark of the cubilawan cinnamon to perfume the mouth and disguise unpleasant odors. The famous little dancers of the Kampong at the Paris Exposition were abundantly supplied with it.

The resinous substance which flows from the bark of the mastic tree hardens the gums and gives a delicious odor to the breath. It is the tear of the mastic. The Sultanas use it freely.

The Roman dames, if we may give credence to Martial, used toothpicks cut from the wood of the mastic tree.

A mixture of camphor and myrrh (a few drops of each in a glass of water) is excellent as a wash for the mouth and for a gargle, when some little indisposition has affected the breath. If myrrh alone is used, ten drops will be sufficient.

After eating cutlets *à la Soubise*, or any other dish cooked with onions, take a cup of black coffee, which is an antidote for the repulsive odor imparted by this vegetable to the bronchial tubes. Garlic should never be eaten.

I have been told of a simple remedy, much used and not at all disagreeable, for the distressing annoyance which we are considering : Pulverized charcoal, fifty grammes, powdered white sugar, fifty grammes, good chocolate, 150 grammes ; put the chocolate in a bain-marie, mix in the sugar and charcoal very thoroughly. After cooling on a marble slab, cut the preparation into small squares ; eat three or four of these squares each day.

The Lips.

It would be unpardonable to leave the subject of the mouth without speaking of the lips.

To be beautiful, as an old poet has said, "the lips should be a bright

raspberry color," and the skin fine and
not chapped. Red lips are inharmo-
nious with certain temperaments. All
attempts to make the color more brilliant will only succeed for a moment
and injure the skin. Therefore do not
have recourse to rubbing with alcoholic
mixtures, or to cosmetics ; you will lose
far more than you gain in the end. If
the skin of your pale lips is not fissured,
they may have a certain freshness, a
satiny appearance, which will give them
a charm, despite their pale rose color.
Alcohol, vinegars, and red paint destroy the delicate skin, which is so
much appreciated in a kiss. How
often children say to ladies who kiss
them : " Your lips prick me," because
the skin is rough.

Many women bite their lips just before entering a drawing-room. Besides

the fact that the color thus produced lasts but a moment, frequent biting makes the lips tender, and predisposes them to chapping.

If the lips are naturally dry and rough, rub them slightly, at night, with equal parts of water and glycerine.

Do not pass the tongue over the lips. It is contrary to the law of good breeding, and the moisture is injurious.

Fever blisters are most disfiguring. If they appear, touch them lightly with powdered alum and they will soon be cured.

To preserve pretty lips constant simpering should be avoided, also grimacing, and all bad habits of the mouth (many persons screw up the mouth and push out the lips in speaking). I once knew a seamstress who forced her lips out at every stitch she took. It is easily understood that unseasonable laughter, contortion, any habit, deforms the mouth and gives the appearance of old age ; but on the other hand, many a dowager remains pretty because she knows how to keep the freshness of her lips and the charm of her smile.

To reduce thick lips, rub them with tannin.

Lip Salve.

When the lips have been chapped by cold or wind, it is easy to cure the trifling annoyance and banish the temporary disfigurement. Here are a few formulæ for salves which are very good in such cases :

First. Pure wax, twelve grammes; olive oil, sixty-six grammes. Melt the wax on a slow fire ; add the oil, mixing thoroughly. Perfume with a few drops of tincture of benzoin. Allow it to cool.

Second. White wax, oil of sweet almonds, essence of rose, and a little carmine.

Third. Sultana Pomatum. White wax, two grammes; spermacetti, two grammes; sweet almond oil, two hundred grammes; rose water, twenty grammes; Peruvian balsam, two grammes. Melt the wax and spermacetti in the oil, in a double boiler; pour into a marble mortar, which has been warmed by hot water; beat thoroughly; add at intervals the rose water, then the balsam, stirring constantly, until the ingredients are mixed and the water no longer separates from the other substances.

Fourth. Sweet almond oil, thirty grammes; spermacetti, four grammes;

white wax, twelve grammes; cocoa butter, four grammes; alkanet, eight grammes. Mix the various ingredients on a slow fire in a double boiler. Strain through muslin. Perfume with essence of rose.

Put these salves into small jars carefully covered or corked.

The Teeth. Care of the Teeth.

"Like pearls, and white as driven snow."

Théophile Gautier speaks somewhere of a dazzling smile of pearls.

It is true that nothing adds so much to the charm of a smile, that nothing is so essential to it, as a double row of white teeth, which are perfectly healthy and are visible behind the lips when these are parted in a smile.

Pretty teeth are the *sine qua non* of

beauty. Good teeth (which is equiva-
lent to saying beautiful teeth) are indispensable to health. " No teeth, no
health," is an aphorism which is strictly
true. It was formulated by a surgeon-
dentist celebrated in France and foreign countries.

The premature loss of teeth makes
the face old before its time. I know
that it is possible to restore to the
mouth "the furniture which it has
lost" (as was said during the eighteenth century), but how annoying is
this necessity !

It is better to carefully preserve the
gift which Nature has bestowed upon
us. Let us take care of our teeth, to
prevent being disfigured by the loss of
them, to escape from dangerous diseases, to avoid the terrible sufferings
imposed by decayed teeth, to preserve

sweetness of breath, which is one of the greatest of charms.

Cleanliness is one of the surest means for overcoming the causes which lead to the destruction of the teeth. They should be carefully brushed night and morning ; it is a good practice to rinse the mouth after each meal if possible ; the particles of food which lodge between the teeth decompose and cause, sooner or later, the abominable tartar which is so fatal to teeth.

Some persons use cold water in cleansing the teeth and rinsing the mouth. I advise warm water for both purposes. One should use an infusion of mint or the following mixture : Three grammes of borax and nine grammes of pure glycerine in a quart of warm water. The first and more simple wash is the better.

The toothbrush should be small, almost round, to reach properly every corner of the mouth. Later on we will mention the dentifrices and powders which we know to be harmless. The greater number of articles of this kind, and some of the most widely advertised, only serve to hasten the loss of the teeth. Some of them are efficacious, and their formulæ we will give.

It is sufficient to brush the teeth with soap two or three times each week (without interfering with the daily cleansing). For this purpose it is well to use a very pure soap. I will not conceal the fact that this operation is not agreeable, but one soon becomes accustomed to it, and the consequences are most delightful. Soap contains alkali, and alkalis are highly recommended for the teeth,

They are antiseptic, and where is the mouth that does not require antiseptics? In a word, it removes the deposits on the teeth, which many of the most famous powders do not, except by destroying the enamel which protects them.

Some persons use salt alone, and with good result; they rub and brush the teeth with it, and afterward rinse with warm water. Their teeth are very white, and the gums hard and red. However, I am afraid this treatment would not suit everyone, whereas soap may be used without fear, whatever the teeth or constitution may be.

Teeth should not be brushed too long at a time. Doing this injures the gums, and it is in this way that the teeth are loosened. The upper teeth should be brushed from above downwards (from the gums toward the edges), the lower teeth, from below upwards. The inside of the teeth should be as carefully brushed as the outside.

The gums must be well cared for, for when they are healthy, there is a better chance that the teeth will be healthy also.

When they are soft, the following powder will harden them : Peruvian bark, fifteen grammes ; powdered ratanhia, six grammes; chlorate of potassia, five grammes. These powders should be well mixed so as to form but one, with which the gums should be rubbed three or four times daily.

The gums must be gradually accustomed to vigorous friction. When soft, gums bleed easily. They are strengthened by frequently chewing cress or cochlearia, or by washing them in an infusion of gentian or blackberry leaves, into which are put a few drops of the tincture of Peruvian bark, or cologne.

Lemon juice also has excellent effects on gums which are soft, or even where there is ulceration. Dip a little soft brush in the juice, and carefully pass over the sore places without touching the teeth. Painting the gums with a tincture of ratanhia and the tincture of pyrethrum in equal parts is often recommended. Apply at night.

The gums may be touched daily with the following mixture: Tincture of cochlearia, fifty grammes; hydrate of chloral, five grammes. This heroic treatment should be taken only under the advice of a physician.

A decoction of myrrh, tannin, and oak bark is an excellent astringent for tender or bleeding gums.

There are foods which injure the teeth — sugar, sweets, pastry, etc. It is said that radishes and dates are injurious to them, because they are acids. The abuse of acids destroys the enamel of the teeth. Figs, like sugar, relax and soften the gums; oils, natural fats, or grease do them no good.

Be careful not to drink anything very cold immediately after swallowing soup. The teeth will suffer from the violent change of temperature. Breathe through the nose, especially in the winter (a good habit also during summer on account of the lungs). In winter, if the breath is taken through the mouth, the teeth are exposed to a much lower temperature than that of the body. This produces inflammation of the periosteum and the pulp of the teeth, congestion of the mucous membrane, and the secretion of an acid which causes sloughing. It is not necessary to go into a dental disquisition. All reasonable people understand that it is injurious to the teeth to breathe through the mouth, or to sleep with the mouth open, which is often the result of sleeping on the back.

Never touch the teeth with pins, or with any metallic instrument.

"When eating," said an old author, "eat on both sides, that one may give the other a rest."

Toothache.

When suffering from toothache, beware of using the poisonous remedies which are recommended. Creosote, cloves, essence of cinnamon, etc., etc., will perhaps soothe the pain, but will destroy the teeth. Fly to the dentist, and if obliged to wait, use only such remedies as are beyond suspicion. For example: pound some parsley and salt together, make a little ball of it and place it in the ear on the side of the aching tooth. Or moisten the cheek on the affected side with lemon juice. Or place a hot flannel on the cheek.

Dieting also calms aching teeth, and so do warm baths. When the teeth have been set on edge by an acid, seltzer water will relieve the sensation. One of my friends is frequently relieved of violent toothache by following a doctor's prescription, which is to place at the angle of the lower jaw, on the spot where the artery is felt, a poultice composed of flour, the white of an egg, brandy, and mastic.

Toothache may be produced by

the acidity of the saliva, which causes inflammation and irritation of the teeth.

A strong solution of bicarbonate of soda is the best remedy for this kind of toothache. Rinse the mouth well with the solution, and apply a little bicarbonate of soda to the teeth and gums with a brush. When suffering, try this remedy, and if relief is obtained, it is certain that the cause of the toothache has been discovered. Thenceforth, use bicarbonate of soda in brushing the teeth.

Several persons have assured me that they have cured caries of the teeth by the following prescription: Fill the hollow tooth with powdered alum, and the pain disappears as fast as the alum melts in the tooth. Renew the operation as often as the pain returns, until it is entirely relieved, and the caries removed. Caries is due to the destructive action of bits of food detained in hollow teeth. It is well known that alum is an antiseptic.

However, when it is within the bounds of possibility, resort to a good dentist.

Filling the teeth in time, either with amalgam or gold, may preserve them indefinitely and prevent intolerable pain. Any negligence is inexcusable.

Powders, Dentifrices, and Elixirs.

If one is determined to use powders and dentifrices, at least be careful in the selection made. Unless purchased from a well-known manufacturer, I would advise that they be made at home, to insure that no cream of tartar, or calcareous salts (substances which are fatal to the enamel of the teeth and injurious to the purity of the breath) should enter into the composition.

The following are a few recipes, the excellence of which I can guarantee, and which are easily prepared. They are from prescriptions made by physicians and pharmacists :

First. Carbonate of lime, 200 grammes ; powder of Armenian bole, 200 grammes ; powder of magnesia, 50 grammes; powder of pyrethrum root, 25 grammes ; powder of cloves, 25 grammes ; powder of bicarbonate of soda, 20 grammes ; essence of English mint, 5 grammes. Mix carefully.

Second. Powdered Peruvian bark, 10 grammes ; tannin, 10 grammes ; charcoal, 10 grammes. Pulverize in a mortar. Preserve in a porcelain or wooden box.

Third. Precipitated chalk, sixty grammes; orris powder, 30 grammes; pulverized myrrh, 1 gramme, 50 centigrammes. Mix and add: Solution of cocaine, .08 centigramme; oil of eucalyptus, 12 drops; triturate together, mix, sift. This powder is very good for diseased teeth and spongy gums.

A druggist's elixir: Green aniseed, 25 grammes; cloves, 10 grammes; cinnamon, 10 grammes; Peruvian bark, 10 grammes; pyrethrum root, 10 grammes; cochineal, 4 grammes; essence of English mint, 6 grammes; rectified spr. alcohol, 90 per cent., 1 quart. Let these ingredients remain in the alcohol for a month, and then strain through filtering paper.

The following is a prescription recommended by a good dentist, who prefers it to *Eau Botot.*

Thymol, 20 centigrammes ; benzoic acid, 2 grammes, 50 centigrammes ; tincture of eucalyptus, 3 grammes ; water, 350 grammes. Shake the bottle. The mouth should be well rinsed with this water on retiring.

It is during the night that the mouth and teeth are in most danger from fermentation and decay, which proceed more rapidly during slumber. Thanks to this wash, decaying teeth are relieved of the contents of their cavities, and are no longer a source of disease and pain. The active cause is eliminated and made inoffensive.

For summer use, the most delicious and the best dentifrice is the strawberry. It cleans the teeth thoroughly.

It should be crushed on the brush; the teeth then rubbed and rinsed in warm water.

An infusion made of the petals of the pink makes a perfect elixir during the summer time. The pink is an antiseptic.

I would advise that a small crust of bread be eaten after each repast.

Tartar.

Despite washings and dentifrices, tartar is deposited on the cleanest teeth, with few exceptions. Gouty and rheumatic persons will perceive the formation of tartar on their teeth in certain quantities, despite all care.

For other constitutions an energetic brushing will always prevent the appearance of tartar, check its growth, and sometimes destroy it.

Alum is recommended for tartar. Take a slight quantity on a moistened brush and rub the teeth every morning with it for two or three days successively. Rinse the mouth with honey water, to correct the astringency of the alum.

It is often necessary to have recourse to more severe measures to destroy the evil. Dr. Magitot, whose name is famous among practitioners of the dental art, does not hesitate to use instruments to remove hard tartar. Once the patient is in his hands he never releases him until he has entirely removed the stony concretion which has formed on the teeth.

The mouth may be full of blood. You would like to check the operator, but he never stops until you are relieved from this first cause of the destruction of the teeth.

The subsequent treatment is very simple. It is only necessary to let pastilles of chlorate of potassia melt in the mouth, but they must be pastilles which will leave no bad effects, such as are not uncommon.

As for the dark deposit on the teeth, it is perhaps dangerous to remove it by the aid of hydrochloric acid. Many conscientious dentists refuse to do this. Salt may be used to prevent this unpleasant vegetation which affects human teeth, if the infliction becomes too great to be endured.

If the mouth is filled with salt water after the extraction of a tooth, hemorrhage need not be feared.

Children's Teeth.

As soon as the teeth of an infant appear, care should be given them. This is a painful time for the little ones, and also for the mothers, who fear results which are sometimes fatal.

The pain attending the appearance of the first little baby teeth may be mitigated by rubbing the gums with Narbonne honey. It relieves and softens the gums (and at the same time being absorbed by the stomach is soothing to the bowels), and the teeth appear without that pain which often results in convulsions and death. A crust of bread, the root of marshmallow, a rubber ring, are all useful to promote dentition. The importance of paying attention to the teeth of children is plain to everyone. There is a double object, to prevent horrible suffering in the present, which they are too feeble to endure, and to insure them in the future healthy and beautiful teeth.

When the second teeth are cut, there are often injurious influences to be combated. There are more or less chances for the formation of caries, or tartar; care must be taken and counsel sought; and every effort made to prevent the aggravation of the evil.

A good mother will also see to it that the teeth are regular. Dentists, by giving attention in time, can prevent all deformities which may appear.

THE VOICE.

THE ORGAN.

" Like softest music to attending ears."

A SWEET voice is a powerful feminine charm. One also admires fine
masculine voices, which are sonorous
and full.

We should therefore be careful of
this organ which Nature has bestowed
upon us, and improve it if possible.
Coarse, shrill, and harsh voices may be
softened by care and study. A woman
with a peacock voice can never charm.

Speak in a low voice, but distinctly.
Loud speaking denotes ill breeding,
and sometimes shows a domineering
spirit; many people drown the voices
of others in a discussion that they may

themselves attract the more attention. To keep the voice at a proper tone, never call from one end of the room to another, nor from upstairs down, nor at any distance where it becomes necessary for one to shout with all his might, as this coarsens and roughens the voice, and in time ruins it.

There are persons who, when spoken to, pay no attention, either from abstraction or from indifference to anything which may proceed from others. The person who speaks is then obliged to raise the voice and repeat, and thus the habit of speaking loudly is frequently formed.

These things occur in families where but little politeness is observed between those who owe each other as much consideration as is due to outsiders.

One should never cry out under the influence of anger, indignation, or pain. These cries forever destroy the harmony of the vocal chords. Children should be prevented from screaming when at play. When they cry from temper, throw a few drops of water in the face and walk away. This will arrest their crying, which is often dangerous while they are young and frail. A physician thinks he has discovered the means of rendering the voice very soft. He maintains that peroxide of hydrogen will improve both the tone and strength of the voice. He advises its use by tenors, baritones, prime donne, etc., and by ordinary mortals who desire to possess musical voices. He bases his opinion on the fact that peroxide is one of the constituents of the Italian atmosphere and dew, and that to its presence is due the beauty, the fullness, of trans-Alpine organs. This doctor has invented a chemical composition to replace the air of Italy. After inhalation, the voices of those who have experimented, it is claimed, become fuller, clearer, richer, and softer.

Trifling Throat Diseases.

How many voices become hoarse and worn as the result of useless fatigue imposed on them! What a defect to either man or woman is a hoarse, indistinct, disagreeable voice! Very often the misfortune can be prevented, or at least remedied.

But there are cases of hoarseness which arise from circumstances over which we have no control. For example, when occasioned by enlargment of the larynx. This organ must be contracted in order to prevent the emission of those unpleasant hoarse sounds which are so painful to delicate ears. In such cases lemonade, orange-ade, the acidulated water of verjuice are excellent where cold drinks are recommended. The throat may also be gargled with equal parts of water and verjuice. If the hoarseness originates in a bronchial affection or slight quinsy, a syrup of hedge mustard (*Sasybrium officinal.*) is used as a gargle. This plant is also a tonic and a pectoral.

In all cases of hoarseness it is well to speak as little as possible, or in very low tones. Water made from pearled barley and cassis jelly are said to be excellent for this troublesome ailment.

Nero drank the water from leeks to

keep his voice in good condition. The onion would have the same effect on our vocal organs. A pippin baked in its skin is highly recommended to orators, and, as is well known, many singers swallow, or are supposed to swallow, the yellow of a raw egg before breakfast each day in order to clear the voice.

Buttermilk is very refreshing when the voice is fatigued.

Tobacco, alcohol, all violent stimulants, are injurious to the voice. Heating food, spices, and condiments should be avoided by those who care to preserve the flexibility of their voices.

Remedies for Clearing the Voice.

The Arabs have a most agreeable remedy for the loss of voice. The person afflicted is nourished exclusively on the pulp of apricots until a cure is effected. They are cooked in the usual way and dried in the sunshine of the Sahara desert.

A gargle of salt water is recommended for a slight irritation of the throat and vocal chords.

Inhaling the vapor arising from hot milk, in which ripe figs have been boiled, gives sweetness to the voice.

Fumigations are excellent. Mix a little amber and pulverized myrrh, throw the powder on a hot shovel, and inhale the fumes.

An infusion of veronica and sugar candy is recommended. Take a small glass before eating.

THE EYES.

" For where is any author in the world
Teaches such beauty as a woman's eye."

SOME eyes are so beautiful that they
atone for all irregularities of the features, and even physical defects.

The beauty of the eye lies in its expression, whether it has borrowed its
color from the corn flower, or shines
like the black diamond, or reflects the
blue of a May sky, or is veiled under
long dark eyelashes.

It should reflect a soul, which is
strong and great, tender and sweet,
loyal and true, ardent and loving. The
inner being should shine through.
" Such harmony is in immortal souls."

When the eye expresses nothing, it is because the spirit is asleep, stupefied. Lustreless eyes never awaken deep and profound sympathy in others; they never conquer hearts or intellects; they have no power.

The poets have equally praised blue eyes and gray, hazel and black, soft and lustrous, flashing and brilliant. The eye demands certain conditions for beauty; it should be long, almond-shaped, and fringed with long lashes. It should be well opened, with a direct, frank expression, a look which dares meet any eye. Not that we condemn the timid glance of a young girl, who turns away astonished and frightened at the admiring gaze of a stranger; but the furtive glance which seeks to avoid the eyes of others. It is well to teach children to look into the faces of

those who speak to them, not inso-
lently, but simply, with the confidence
which all honest persons should feel in
themselves and others. It is wrong to
repress eagerness, enthusiasm, in young
creatures when it is excited by the
beautiful, the great, and the good. If
they are forced to restrain the excitement in their young blood, if their
hearts are not permitted to beat freely,
they will veil the fire in their glances,
and their eyes will lose all frankness of
expression.

Truly beautiful eyes are those
which express feelings without concealment. I have seen sweet, tender, and
kind eyes flash lightning glances in
moments of indignation or admiration.
They know nothing of concealment.
Those who have such eyes may be
trusted,

Beware of the man who does not look you clearly in the eye. He has possibilities of evil in his nature. There are eyes which are luminous, others which seem to be veiled behind a curtain.

Men and women of the world are accustomed to judge human nature by the expression of the eye. Many people read character by the eyes, and can thus distinguish the false from the loyal, the frank from the deceitful, the hard from the tender, the energetic from the indolent, the sympathetic from the indifferent.

Love speaks through the eyes, and needs no other language. " Love," says an English poet, " is born in the eyes." Unfortunately he adds in a jesting spirit, "like the potato," alluding to the eyes of that vegetable which form its roots.

How often have we heard " One
look from her eyes enchained me forever." Beautiful limpid eyes so ap-
peal to heart and soul that they are
irresistible.

The power of the hypnotist lies
chiefly in the eyes. It is a power
which should never be abused.

To my mind, no eyes can be beautiful unless they reflect good wholesome
thoughts and noble sentiments. Generous indignation does not destroy
their seductive power, and their beauty
is not lessened by the fire of enthusiasm.

The most perfectly colored and well-
shaped eyes, under the influence of
jealousy, deceit, envy, or brutal anger,
lose all their charms.

Women who " make eyes " do not
deserve to have eyes.

Care of the Eyes.

Never rub the eyes, for this practice causes inflammation of the lids, and however beautiful the expression, if the eyes are red or without lashes, they lose their charm.

When a foreign substance gets into the eye do not irritate it by trying to force it out. Keep the eye closed for a few moments, or until the object is removed by the tears which will flow.

If the wind has reddened the eyelids, wash them in slightly salted warm water (common salt). Veils, especially dotted ones, are very injurious to the eyes. They should, therefore, only be used during the winter, as a protection against cold.

Late hours and artificial light redden and fatigue the eyes. Lamps should be supplied with shades. It is dangerous to gaze at the sun or electric light. Gaslight, candles, ordinary lamps, should be shaded by screens, smoked glasses, etc.

Never sit in front of a blazing fire without a screen.

Reflections of light on white walls, or on long stretches of dusty road, or on snow, are very fatiguing to the eyes when not protected by smoked glasses; some oculists insist that even these glasses are injurious. Hats with large brims, shading the brow, make the best head covering for summer wear, as they shade the eye from the painfully bright rays of light.

However strong the eyes may be, give them a little rest after a few hours' continuous use. Never force them to gaze at minute objects when they are weak; neither write, read, nor sew when the light is dim. During all continuous work close the eyes from time to time at intervals.

The most reposeful colors to the eyes are blue and green. Do not surround yourself with very bright colors. Red is blinding. Choose in preference delicate colors in draperies, stuffs, paper, etc.

Dark tints are not suitable in decoration or furniture. Too great contrast between colors is equally fatiguing to the sight.

The light should fall from the side, not full in the face. When working it should be allowed to fall upon the left side. Writing should be done on tinted paper, and only well printed books and papers should be read. Never read, write, or sew lying down, as it is apt to produce vertigo. It is bad to read on the railway, in a carriage, while walking, in bed, while physically tired, and also when convalescent. Be careful of your stomach. It is said that Milton became blind, not only from over-use of his eyes, but from dyspepsia. Living in damp places produces feebleness of vision. Hygienic conditions, sobriety, the avoidance of all excesses are rewarded by good eyesight.

Insufficient nourishment is very injurious. Avoid passing from extremes of heat and cold, from obscurity into light. Beds should not be so placed that the eyes receive the full rays of sunlight on awakening. The light should fall from the side. It is well to wait a few moments on coming from an obscure light into a bright one, before beginning to read, write, or work. Montaigne advises the placing of a colorless glass on the page which is being read, and in this way the wearing of spectacles may be avoided indefinitely. Under the glass, the paper of the book or magazine is, in fact, softened, and the characters appear more clearly. The light should not be allowed to strike directly on the glass.

Never rub the eyes on awakening, and do not permit children to acquire the habit.

Use eyeglasses, microscopes, magnifying glasses, as little as possible. Remove your spectacles or eyeglasses often in walking, talking, etc.

Bathe the eyes frequently, especially night and morning. If congestion is feared, use warm water. Weak, black tea is good for pain in the eyes.

Avoid all ointments, washes, etc., not prescribed by a good physician or oculist. It is impossible too strongly to denounce the use of so-called "eye beautifiers." Many women have ruined their eyes from just such folly.

If the eyelids are inflamed, wash them in rosewater and plantain. The juice of the strawberry strained through a piece of linen is very efficacious.

An old physician has advised the use of elderberry water for the painful itching sometimes felt in the eyes.

The water of Chervil is refreshing to irritated eyes. A physician recommends the following prescription : One quart of soft water, a pinch of common salt, a spoonful of brandy. Allow it to dissolve. Shake well before using. This wash will strengthen the sight and restore its powers.

Night is the best time for bathing the eyes.

Eyelashes.

To be beautiful and to protect properly the eye, the lashes should be long and thick. When they possess these qualities, they soften the expression.

It is asserted that there is a salve called trikogene which makes the lashes grow. Some women have their lashes trimmed by an expert to make them longer and thicker. The eye should never be rubbed. This habit, which is evil in many respects, causes the lashes to fall out. I would advise that they should not be blackened, though it adds to the charm of the eye. All artificial coloring so near this precious organ of sight is doubly dangerous.

Eyebrows.

Heavy eyebrows impart a brutal and rough expression to the face. Small fine brushes are made to keep them in order. Penciled, well-arched eyebrows give to the face an air of serenity. On the other hand moderately thick eyebrows are an improvement to the eyes.

Scant, thin eyebrows, which form a red line above the eye, are a blemish. They can be improved by applying a little petroleum oil every morning after having bathed them in cold water. Clipping the eyebrows makes them thicker.

To those who insist on artificially lengthening and coloring the eyebrows, despite my horror of dyeing, I suggest a means which is perfectly harmless :

it is a solution of Chinese ink and rose water. This is one of the secrets of the harem.

Other Counsels.

It is affirmed that squinting is frequently due to placing the cradle of an infant in a bad light. The child on awakening is forced to look cross-eyed. Consequently the child's bed should be carefully situated. The light should strike it always from the side, and never from in front or behind the head. Squinting is easily corrected, and often corrects itself. In obstinate cases I urge those who are afflicted to consult a good oculist. Time, money, suffering, even, should influence no one who desires relief. The good results will amply recompense all sacrifices.

THE NOSE.

"If the nose of Cleopatra had been shorter, the whole face of the earth would have been changed."

YOUR nose may be perfectly chiseled, but if the roses on your cheek invade it, you would prefer a snub nose that is white to an inflamed Grecian one. You would be quite right if there were no remedy for this evil.

When the redness of the nose is not due to cold weather, but to the dryness of the nasal passage or to the delicacy of the capillary vessels, it is easy to remove the inflammation. The following wash may be used: Powdered borax, ten grammes; one teaspoonful of cologne; soft water, 150 grammes. Melt the borax in the water; then add the cologne. It is sufficient to moisten the nose with the wash and let it dry without wiping. When it begins to burn again, the treatment should be renewed.

Here is another and similar wash: Dissolve two grammes of borax in fifteen grammes of rose water, and as much orange flower water. Moisten the nose three times each day with this refreshing wash.

Redness of the nose arises frequently from congestion. In this case it should be washed only at night, before going to bed, and in hot water.

This unbecoming redness which we are discussing may also be attributable to the temperament. Scrofulous persons are afflicted with it. They should abstain from ham, fat of any kind, meat, bacon, grease; also salt meats and spiced food.

This redness is sometimes produced by the condition of the nostrils, which swell. For this use hot water; cold water increases the redness of the nose. The nostrils should never be touched with the fingers. Draw into them a little warm water and then eject it gently. Récamier cream spread on the irritated parts will protect them from the effects of the air, and soften the inflamed surface. A cold in the head aggravates the evil, in which case the head should be covered when sleeping. Tight clothes, especially corsets, and a too feeble action of the heart cause this redness. In the first case, the clothes must be loosened. In the second, much rest should be indulged in. In the morning on rising bathe the body in cold water and rub vigorously with a Turkish bath brush. The air breathed should be pure, both night and day.

Acne, or Blackheads.

Blackheads are a form of acne, indicated by little black specks on the skin, chiefly about the nose, forehead, and chin. Each speck marks an obstructed outlet of the sebaceous glands, and if pressure is made on either side, something having the appearance of a small white worm may be pressed out. Upon careful examination this so-called worm proves to be a mass of hardened sebaceous matter, or sebum, which has assumed this shape by being pressed through the small outlet of the follicle. The black speck giving to this little cylinder of fat the appearance of a head, is, shocking as it is, simply an accumulation of dirt. The technical term for one of these little masses is comedo. When examined under a microscope they are frequently found to contain a whole family of parasites; male, female, and their numerous progeny.

Obviously there is but one way of getting rid of blackheads, and that is by forcing them out of the clogged pore. They cannot be drawn back from whence they came, and in pressing them out before the skin is properly softened and prepared for their ejection the patient ruptures the delicate tissue, causing either an ugly little scar, or more likely an enlargement of the opening, which immediately fills up again, each time increasing in size and more malignant in appearance.

Blackheads may not only be removed without leaving any scar, but once rid of them the patient need never again be troubled with them, if he will but carefully follow the advice here given.

For three weeks, or until the skin is thoroughly softened, apply Récamier cream every night before retiring. Let the cream remain on the face during the night. In the morning wash it off with water, as hot as can pleasantly be borne, and a little pure soap. Rinse the face thoroughly with cooler water. At the end of three weeks the blackheads will, in most cases, have been expelled by the treatment. In obstinate cases proceed as follows :

Before attempting the removal of these truly loathsome blemishes, apply a little Récamier cream. Press on

either side of the clogged pore until
the so-called "worm" is forced out.
Be careful not to be rough and injure
the skin by sharp finger nails or any
steel instrument ; if the sebaceous matter will not come out it is because the
skin is not properly softened, and you
must patiently continue the first part
of the treatment. Operate on the
blackheads at night, if possible, before
retiring, and do not attempt to get rid
of all at one time. After the matter is
forced out bathe the face in warm
water, in which put a little pulverized
borax, and also use a little pure soap
that the now emptied follicle may be
thoroughly cleansed. Continue this
treatment until the blackheads are all
gone.

Do not imagine, however, that these
troublesome imperfections will not re-

turn if you neglect your skin. Nothing but care will keep the follicle from filling up again, care and great cleanliness.

The Science of Rhinoplasty.

This science concerning the nose has reached such perfection that it is now possible to modify or change the form of the nose. The process employed is due to discoveries in the medical profession.

Those persons afflicted with large noses may be glad to learn of a method of reducing their proportions. Wear eyeglass frames during the night, and as much as possible during the day. If the nose is slightly crooked—deviating from the median line—it should be blown exclusively on the defective side until it becomes perfectly straight.

In New York some millionaires *
change their noses into either Greek,
Roman, or Hebrew, as they prefer, by
means of an instrument which they
wear at night.

* The European idea of the " New York millionaire " is
a caricature, as distorted as the typical Yankee of the stage.
—H. H. A.

THE EAR.

" Like shells of pearly hue."

I MUST be pardoned if I insist on the cleansing of the external ear, as well as of the auditory passage, which is also external. There are persons who are scrupulously clean, but who from ignorance of the details of this part of the body use a sponge, or merely a towel, in cleansing the ear, and so do not succeed in removing the accumulations of dust or other particles which may be secreted in the folds. A little instrument of ivory called an aurilave is necessary. It must be covered with the end of a wet towel, and penetrate into all the folds and corners, which have first been soaped, and where the fingers, no matter how slender, cannot reach. Remove from the external passage the wax, which accumulates in too great quantities and is disgusting to the eye.

I have seen charming little shell-shaped ears, with rosy tips, but which were disgraced by want of care. They should have been adorable, but were repulsive. How much worse an ugly ear must appear when neglected!

Precautions against Deafness.

If there is ever so slight a tendency to deafness, care should be taken not to wet the hair. Avoid cold plunge baths. Wear even in the bath an oil silk cap.

When the ear is slightly deaf never

allow the feet to grow cold. Avoid dampness of the extremities, and never sit with the back to an open window. These imprudences aggravate the infirmity.

Never pour any liquid into the ear, unless it has first been warmed. Never pour oil, or milk, or any other greasy substance into it with the hope of relieving it when suffering from ear-ache. All grease becomes rancid and increases the inflammation.

If a living insect gets into the ear there is no cause for alarm, for the bitter cerumen will soon force it to leave.

Hot water may be poured into the canal of the ear and the insect will be drowned and come to the surface. A few puffs of smoke blown into the ear will stupefy the intruder.

Never strike a child on the ear. The tympanum might thus be ruptured, and incurable deafness be the result of the brutal act.

The Acoustic Fan.

I wish to point out to women who are afflicted with a nervous form of deafness an extremely simple and easy way of getting rid of this disagreeable infirmity, which almost excludes from society those who are afflicted by it, preventing their hearing conversations around them, and consequently from taking any part in them.

They should carry a Japanese fan, made of bamboo sticks, thick and covered with paper. When they wish to listen they have but to take the fan, open it, apply the rim to the upper jaw (on the side of the defective ear) and bend it sufficiently to give some tension to the bamboo sticks. They will be quite surprised to find that they can hear as well as though they used an audiphone or dentaphone. Besides, this fan is a less formidable and more graceful appliance.

THE HAND.

ITS BEAUTY.

" I take thy hand, this hand,
As soft as dove's down and as white as it."

IT is asserted that one must be of patrician descent for five generations to possess hands so perfect and aristocratic as to be beyond criticism.

I cannot say that this recipe is infallible ; 'it is certain that it is not within the reach of all.

Still there is consolation. It is a great deal to have a white and delicate hand, though not perfectly modeled, and this at least is possible, even while doing housework, or gardening, on condition, however, that some pains be taken.

Never hesitate then to use the hands when necessary, to utilize the gifts which God has given you for the service of others. It is easy to keep them soft and fine, despite the work you may be forced to do. The noble women of other days attached so much importance to the beauty of their hands that one of them, the Countess of Soissons, never closed hers for fear of hardening the joints. How could any woman condemn herself to such torture? It was for the same reason that pages, and later lackeys, were required to carry prayer-books and other small articles which were considered too heavy for slender and small hands. In the 18th century fashionable women required their servants to open the doors for them lest their hands should be made large by the handles, and also

by the weight of the door. They cited
Madame Crequy as a surprisingly reso-
lute woman, "because," said they, "if
no lackey were within call, she opened
the doors herself, without fear of blis-
tering her hands."

In our day feminine hands are more
useful. Many women do not shrink
from manipulating potter's clay, and
we do homage to those who hold in
horror the idleness in which their ancestors found pleasure.

If the hands are afflicted with wens
or warts they may be removed by
means of the remedies suggested in
the chapter on the face.

Care of the Hands.

In doing housework or gardening,
old gloves which have lost their freshness and grown large by use may be

worn.   They will protect the hands
from the effects of the air, and keep
them clean.   Too frequent washing is
open to objection.   But there are
many labors which cannot be performed
with covered hands, and in that case
they must be washed as often as necessary.   A perfectly pure soap should
be used.   A little almond meal may
be put into the warm water in which
the hands are washed, and if they are
much soiled a little borax or ammonia
may be added.

The roughest hands will be softened
if care is given them before retiring
at night.   It scarcely requires five
minutes to efface the traces which the
rudest labor may have left on the
hands.   And the necessary articles are
not expensive.   A nail brush, a box
of rose paste, a box of nail powder, a

vial of ammonia, almond meal, and
French Amandine and a lemon are
useful.

If a callous spot forms on the inside
of the hand it must be rubbed, as
patiently and for as long a time as
may be necessary, with pumice stone.
This operation preserves the softness
of the hand. and the delicacy of
touch.

Stains may be removed by lemon,
borax, or ammonia, according to their
nature.

When the hands have been perfectly cleansed, rub them with French
Amandine. Wear gloves while sweep-
ing.

If glycerine were not injurious to
many skins it would be excellent. The
following mixture will be acceptable
to those who can use glycerine. The

yolk of an egg, six grammes of glycerine, seven grammes of borax. Mix well. Rub the hands with this salve, and cover them with gloves.

Almond meal, which is cheaper, will do as well. The white of an egg is recommended, in which has been dissolved five centigrammes of alum.*

If the hands are very rough, and have been much used, cold cream may be employed with great advantage at the beginning of the daily treatment which has been suggested. After using for one month the hands will be sufficiently improved to need only almond meal.

Women who do no domestic work may keep their hands white by simply washing them night and morning in bran water.

---

* Alum often roughens the skin. Use it carefully, if at all.—H. H. A.

A mixture of lemon juice and glycerine, equal parts, is frequently advised for redness of the hands. The following is a recipe for almond paste : Take fifty grammes of bitter almonds; throw into boiling water in order to remove the skins; dry them. Crush in a mortar or with a thick bottle. Crush separately thirty grammes of orris root (if the skin is not easily irritated), and thirty grammes of starch. Mix with the pounded almonds, and add the yolks of four eggs. Moisten the paste with 200 grammes of spirits of wine, and twenty drops of essence of rose. Heat on a very slow fire, stirring incessantly with a spoon. This preparation should be kept in jars in a cool place. It becomes a powder, and is used to rub the hands night and morning. This paste may also be made of bitter almonds, 250 grammes; oil of sweet almonds, 500 grammes; honey, 500 grammes; the yolks of six eggs. The honey is heated separately; then mix with the flour and eggs. Add the oil last, and knead the whole.

Washing the Hands During the Day.

Never have soiled hands, but do not wash oftener than necessary. Lemon juice will remove many stains. If a little salt is added to this juice it is still more efficacious.

A bit of orange or lemon skin removes tar stains. Care must be taken to wipe the hands dry immediately.

Fresh tomatoes and strawberries, a leaf of sorrel, a little milk, are also excellent for removing ink stains.

Before peeling Irish potatoes, the hands should be well dried, and should not be washed immediately after. By this slight precaution they will not be stained with the juice of the tuber.

After paring certain fruits and vegetables a little lemon juice removes all stain. The hands must first be moistened in water.

To cleanse the hands after very rough work use a good emollient or cream. Rub the hands with a small quantity of the emollient, which will penetrate well into the pores of the skin and become incorporated with the greasy substances. Wash the hands in hot water and soap. This treatment makes them very soft.

Hands which are "sanctified by labor" may thus retain an agreeable appearance, which is not to be disdained, especially when it is so easily obtained.

Moist Hands.

Moist hands are unfit for certain kinds of work, and are unpleasant to the touch.

To keep the hands agreeably dry, rub the palms several times each day with a cloth soaked in the following preparation : Cologne water, seventy grammes ; tincture belladonna, fifteen grammes.

Hands which have a tendency to perspire too freely when exposed to the slightest heat may be washed in water in which a little powdered alum has been dissolved.

Sunburned Hands.

At the close of summer, hands which have been kissed too often by the sun are a source of annoyance. The present rage for out-of-door sports, such as croquet, lawn tennis, sailing and rowing, has played havoc with many fair hands. The sunburned hand is in harmony with the life led in summer. On returning to town and resuming laces and silks the contrast is not pleasing. One is tempted too late to regret not having worn gloves.

Time is a certain cure for sunburn. When it is impossible to wait there are other remedies which it may be well to try : lemon juice and glycerine mixed, or a paste made of corn starch and glycerine. A farmer's daughter of my acquaintance uses only buttermilk. The acidity is said to remove freckles and sunburn ; the oil contained in it is singularly beneficial and softening to the skin. It is as efficacious as any remedy known, especially if the hands are washed in it on going to bed and then covered with gloves. Many persons wash their hands only in hot water during the day. At night they moisten them with rose water and glycerine, and wear gloves while sleeping.* All the preparations recommended, in the chapter devoted to the face, for sunburn and freckles, are equally applicable to the hands.

Large Hands.

If the hands are large do not wear tight sleeves. The pressure on the arm will make the hands swell. A tight wrist band is as unbecoming to a large hand as a low heel is to a large foot.

* It is unpleasant to wear gloves all night, and unnecessary. There are many simple and excellent emollients which will keep the hands soft and smooth without wearing gloves. —H. H. A.

If the fingers are square or very large at the ends they may be made more tapering by continuous pinching and pressing. It is unnecessary to say that taper fingers, which are so coveted, cannot be secured in a day, but with time improvement will be noticed.

Chapped Hands.

For children, and even for many grown persons, winter is the time for chapped hands. It requires but little care to avoid the suffering which results from chapped skin. It is essential that the hands should be thoroughly dried each time they are washed, and never exposed, when moist, either to cold or to the heat of the fire.

Women who are occupied with household cares, who paint, or are engaged in similar occupations, are

obliged to wash their hands frequently, and in order to save time they
are often careless about drying them ;
the result is a rough, red skin. Never
neglect to dry your hands as thoroughly as possible. They may also
be manipulated before the fire until
soft and flexible.

Children should be taught to dry
the hands in this manner.

It is painful to look at the tiny chapped hands of most of the little girls
and boys whom you meet. The little
creatures suffer both from cold and
artificial heat. With proper care the
hands may be inured to great artificial
extremes of temperature.

Rubbing the hands with amandine
before retiring preserves them from
the disastrous effects of cold or heat
to which they may have been sub-

jected. They must not be washed in cold water, as this predisposes them to chapping. Very hot water is not good for them either. People who have not moist skins should be especially careful to dry the hands thoroughly after washing. They may afterward be covered with cold cream or amandine, which should be wiped off with a soft towel.

Where these precautions are not taken and the hands are neglected, a cure may be effected by the following treatment : Wash the hands in hot water and anoint them well with amandine, honey paste, or cold cream. Rub the hands together, interlacing the fingers, until they become soft and are no longer easily hurt when struck against any hard substance. Afterward it will be necessary to remove the grease by washing them in warm water with a few drops of ammonia and a pure soap. Change the water several times, Then apply to the hands the following mixture : Glycerine, cologne, soft water, equal parts. After this process the hands will be soft and not at all greasy or sticky, as might be supposed. I have seen a laundress whose hands seemed to have been parboiled by continual washing of clothes. She suffered greatly, and the stretched, corroded skin of her poor hands was as painful as that of the face often becomes, when it has been too frequently steamed. By using the prescription above referred to her hands became supple and white. An English physician recommends the following mixture to preserve delicate hands from chapping : Carbonic acid, seven

grammes, fifty centigrammes ; glycerine, ten grammes ; yolk of one egg.
Mix well. Anoint the hands several
times each day. If there is the least
scratch on the skin do not use this remedy. Here are a few other recipes for
this painful trouble. They are equally
serviceable for any part of the
body :

First. Yellow wax, fifteen grammes ;
olive oil, twenty grammes. Cut the wax
into small pieces, throw it into the oil,
and melt over a slow fire in a Puritan
Cooker saucepan. Rub the chapped
places every night with this pomade.
If it is the hands which are affected,
wear gloves ; if other parts of the
body, use a bit of old linen.

Second. Cocoa butter, five
grammes ; oil of sweet almonds, five
grammes ; oxide of zinc, eight

grammes, ten centigrammes; borate of soda, ten centigrammes; essence of bergamot, eight drops. This liniment is very good for the lips also.

Third. Take one handful of ground flax seed (very pure), one spoonful of oil of bitter almonds; mix well, and add a sufficient quantity of hot water to form a thin paste. Put the hands in this paste and rub them for about fifteen minutes. Afterward rinse in warm water. The oil of bitter almonds is prepared by mixing two grammes of essence of bitter almond in 500 grammes of olive oil. This recipe may also be used to soften the skin of the hands and to remove chilblains which are not bleeding—another winter ailment which we will now consider.

Chilblains.

Chilblains are still more to be feared than chapping. A feeble temperament and bad nourishment are often the causes of this affection. One should walk a great deal, use the hands freely, rub the chilblain parts which are not bleeding with alcholic preparations, and keep hands and feet very warm.

One would suppose the hands less delicate and less in need of covering than the face. However, everyone knows the necessity of protecting them from the biting cold of frost or wind.

In damp and mild winters chilblains are most painful. There are many remedies for this trouble, which is not dangerous, but the cause of great suffering, and which will deform the prettiest hands in the world.

First. Pound the bulbs of lilies and place them in a vase containing nut oil. Apply this liniment on the sore places, and cover with a soft cloth. (This is excellent.)

Second. Brittany honey will cicatrize open chilblains. Anoint the parts affected, and cover with a soft white cloth.

Third. Poultice the hands at night; rub with the following mixture in the morning: Tincture benzoin, sixty grammes; honey, thirty grammes; water, 210 grammes. Mix well.

Fourth. Wash ulcerated chilblains with tincture of myrrh diluted with warm water.

Fifth. Anoint cracked chilblains with Sultana pomatum, and cover with a soft, fine cloth. Cracked chilblains are difficult to cure in winter. This painful stage of the disease may be prevented by using the following prescriptions, which should never be applied to chilblains when bleeding.

First. Saturate the parts frequently with a little spirits of salt put into a large quantity of water. (Linnée.)

Second. A physician recommends a solution of permanganate of potassium to destroy the chilblain.*

Third. Another prescribes the following treatment: before going to bed bathe the hands in mustard and water, then apply a liniment composed of camphor and turpentine oil.

Fourth. Constipation must be avoided, and the body should perform all its functions. Avoid wearing tight sleeves, which impede circulation, make

* This should be used with discretion. It may give much pain.—H. H. A.

the hands cold, and produce chilblains. They are sometimes prevented by rubbing the hands with a slice of lemon. (This is also good for chapping.)

Fifth. Infuse thirty peppers in double their weight of rectified spirits, keep in a warm place for one week, and you will thus obtain a strong tincture. In another vessel, melt some gum Arabic in water, making it the consistency of syrup; the quantity should equal that of a tincture. Mix the two preparations, stirring well, until they become cloudy, opaque. Take some leaves of tissue paper, cover the surface of the sheet with the mixture, and allow it to dry; place a second sheet over the first; if the surface is brilliant after the second drying the two applications will be sufficient. If not, apply once more. The paper which is thus prepared is intended (when moistened) to cure red, swollen, or burning fingers.

Sixth. Wash in mustard water. Put some mustard (Dijon preferred) in hot water, and apply.

Seventh. One-half part of sulphuric acid, two of glycerine, and three of water. Have this prepared by a druggist. The vial should be labeled poison. Wash the afflicted parts in this water.

Eighth. Salts of ammonia, one ounce; glycerine, one and a half ounce; rose water, eight ounces; shake well until the ingredients are dissolved and mixed. Use as a wash.

Ninth. Wash the hands two or three times each week with a saline solution.

Tenth. Cut two white turnips in

slices and pass through the sieve with three large spoonfuls of pure animal fat. Apply at night and cover with white cloth.

Eleventh. Infuse one handful of oak bark in warm water, and let the hands soak in it for a few minutes.

Twelfth. Make a decoction of a pinch of laurel leaves in one quart of water. Wash the hands each morning in this water, which should be warm.

Thirteenth. At the first signs of redness and irritation use the following mixture: Five parts of essence of rosemary and one part spirits of wine.

Fourteenth. Make a lotion with ninety grammes spirits of wine at ninety degrees, into which melt ten grammes of phenic acid, crystallized. Apply with a cloth tampon. At night put on a compress.

Vinegar added to one-quarter part of camphorated brandy prevents chilblains on hands which are susceptible to this trouble.

All the remedies recommended for the hands may also be used for chilblains on the feet.

Care of the Nails.

Pretty nails are considered a great beauty. At the base there should be a white crescent and the nails should be as rosy as the dawn. Beautiful nails are compared by the poets to onyx, and, in fact, in Greek onyx means nail. According to the mythological legend : " One day Love, finding Venus asleep, cut her nails with the iron point of his arrow and flew off. The clippings fell on the sands of the shore, and, as nothing which comes from the body of an immortal can perish, the Fates carefully gathered them up and changed them into the quasi-precious stones which are called onyx." *

The nails should be cut in a curve which follows the shape of the end of the finger. The surface of the nails should also be polished.

One hour a week spent in caring for the nails is sufficient to keep them in

---

* The "Art of Manicuring" was originated by Sitts, who was Louis Phillipe's pedicure. His descendants are still famous in France, and the Sitts method undoubtedly is the proper and scientific one. The Sitts method totally condemns the use of steel either under or around the nail. Madame Sitts says, "An orange-wood stick with a little French amandine will keep the nails perfectly smooth and clean underneath. Why roughen them with a piece of sharp steel, or thicken them with an acid? And as for cutting and lacerating the cuticle around the outside of the nail, why that was intended by nature as a selvage (lisiere) and if you cut it you make them ragged just as you would the selvage of a bit of cloth. As well cut the border of the eyelid or ear." The Sitts method is practiced by one or two manicures in New York.—H. H. A.

good order, if they are rubbed and cleaned carefully each day.

Never use a steel instrument in cleaning the nails, as it hardens them and causes the dust to accumulate beneath. Nothing is better than the juice of a lemon, which keeps the skin at the base from encroaching on the nail and also prevents white spots, often caused by lack of care. Cold cream at night, or French amandine, is excellent for softening the nails, and also prevents them from breaking off and becoming dull.

I have been given a recipe for making the nails hard. (The hardness of a nail is one of the conditions of its beauty.) Melt on a very slow fire fifteen grammes of nut oil, two grammes and fifty centigrammes of white wax, five grammes of rosin, and one gramme

of alum.   This pomatum, which should
be whipped while on the fire, is to be
used at night.

A manicure set is indispensable for
the proper care of the nails.   It should
consist of an ordinary nail brush, a
still smaller one to go under the nail,
a file, a polishing brush, curved scissors
—a pair for each hand ; the nails of the
right hand cannot be cut with scissors
made for cutting the nails of the left
hand.

Gloves.

If the gloves do not fit easily, the
hands appear short and clumsy.   The
fingers of the glove should be quite as
long as the fingers of the hand.

Besides, tight gloves do not last,
which is an economical consideration.
Refined and thoroughbred women

never wear gloves too small for them,
and many insist on a glove large
enough to *wrinkle*, which may be taken
off or put on in an instant. Kid gloves
wear much longer when they are properly put on the first time. " It is quite
a science," said a charming woman.
The hand should be perfectly clean, dry
and cool. Never put on gloves when
the hands are moist or too warm.

First push in the four fingers, leaving
the thumb out and the rest of the
glove turned back over the hand.
When the fingers are on, thanks to the
gentle movements of the other hand,
draw on the thumb with great care,
placing the elbow on the knee.
After this, draw back the wrist of the
glove and button the second button,
continuing this all the way up. Then
return to the first button, and you will

see how easily it fastens without cracking the kid, which often happens if
buttoned first.   Besides this, the but-
tonhole will not be stretched, which
is of great importance if one wishes
the glove to look well as long as it
lasts.   Never pull the glove off by the
finger tips, but by the wrists.   They
will thus be turned wrong side out, and
the moisture communicated from the
hand is quickly evaporated.   When
they are dry put them carefully away
in a proper place.   Otherwise they
shrink, split easily, and are useless.
Never roll up gloves.   Place them at
full length in a box or perfumed sachet.
Light gloves should be put away between two pieces of white flannel to
preserve them from contact with dark
gloves, which might stain them.

Black kid gloves are renewed by applying with a feather a few drops of good black ink in a spoonful of olive oil and drying them in the sun. Light gloves, if only slightly soiled, may be cleansed with flour. If much soiled use neufaline.

In buying gloves examine the seams well. If the stitching shows a drawn white place on the kid they will be easily torn, will last only a short time, and never look well.

Silk and woolen gloves are much warmer than kid. For very cold days fur-lined gloves may be used, or woolen gloves drawn over kid ones.

The Arm.

The feminine arm should be round and white. If it is thin it may be developed by rubbing it energetically.

Superfluous hair on the arm may be

removed by the remedies recommended for the face.

Red arms may be rubbed with almond and honey paste.

Cosmetics are not to be recommended (especially for young girls), though some of them are harmless. They should be of some well-known manufacture.

THE FOOT.

CONDITIONS OF BEAUTY.

" The grass stoops not, she treads on it so light."

WHEN the foot is well formed, shoes wear out slowly and the general appearance is harmonious and graceful.

The most charming foot can be deformed by a shoe that is too short or too narrow. An ugly foot becomes still more so if an effort is made to conceal its dimensions by compression. We must resign ourselves to the feet which nature has given us. We endure useless torture when wearing shoes not intended for us, and which, instead of remedying defects, but add to them.

The feet of the ancients were very beautiful (see the statues) because the sandals and buskins did not closely confine them. In our time, it is only in the East, especially in Japan, that the human foot can be seen in all its perfection. In the Empire of the Rising Sun the feet formerly knew no restraint. The foot covering was always made for the comfort of the foot, and followed its outlines. But the custom of the European has been adopted within the land of the Tycoon, and our abominable style of foot covering, which deforms the foot because it regards neither its structure nor the movement made in walking, is used.

Ladies' boots, narrow and pointed shoes, have given rise to innumerable pains and infirmities, and have spoiled both the feet and the general appearance.

Here are a few hints concerning a reasonable coquetry; but will they be heeded? Do not attempt to shorten the foot; this only increases its thickness. There is no beauty in such a foot. It should be well proportioned, and in harmony with the body. A long and slender foot is more elegant because it looks narrower. It is absurd to compress a large foot. It is only made more ugly. It becomes very painful, and all ease in walking is sacrificed.

It is asserted that the English and Germans have very large feet because they drink so much beer. And that Americans, who also drink a great deal of beer, are beginning to lose the beauty of their feet. In the wine countries, France, Spain, Italy, etc., where the women drink but little, the feminine feet are very delicate, very shapely.

Choice of Shoes.

If the slender foot is a little too long, it should be encased in a shoe or boot which has a short vamp, laced or buttoned up the front. When the shoe is ornamented on the front part, the length of the foot is diminished.

If short and fat, the foot requires shoes which have long vamps buttoned or laced on the side.

When the foot is very flat it requires rather high heels.

On the contrary, when the instep possesses that curve which is found in its perfection among the Arabs, and which is considered a proof of blue blood by the Spaniards, this curve should not be exaggerated by a high heel, which shortens a foot that does not need to be shortened.

The Molière shoe enlarges the ankle and breaks the curve ; it should be abandoned, in the name of all that is æsthetic. The low shoe is, on the contrary, very pretty and sensible.

The boot is really not in good taste, though in the winter no other covering is possible, for the feet and ankles must be protected from the cold. The black bottine is the only really pretty covering, and should extend above the ankle. When of cloth it makes the foot appear much larger than when of leather or kid.

A white shoe should never be worn except on a perfect foot, as it increases its size and makes it more conspicuous. Under all circumstances, a shoe should be at least one shade darker than the gown.

Slippers or Oxford ties, but not shoes, may be of any color. They should harmonize with the toilet.

Black shoes and stockings diminish the size of the foot in length and thickness.

Women who have stout ankles should wear high clocked stockings.

It is the worst possible taste to wear heavy shoes with light toilets. If you cannot afford fine shoes, wear only dark and simple gowns.

Trying on Shoes.

If possible have shoes made to order. If you must buy ready-made ones, try them on in the evening. The feet are larger and more sensitive at night, because of the exercise they

have had during the day. The muscles are also more tender from constant motion and the augmented flow
of blood. The weight of the body so
seriously affects the circulation of the
blood that women obliged to stand all
day suffer much from swollen feet.
This, too, often causes varicose veins.
When one is in good health, the feet
return to their normal size after a rest.
This is because they no longer have
to sustain the weight of the body.

Therefore shoes should be tried on
at night (when the feet are tired).
In this way the shoes will be comfortable at all times.

Never wear new shoes when taking
a long walk. Wear them first in the
house for several days, then on short
walks.

In taking the precautions which I

have advised, you will insure as much comfort to your foot in a new shoe as in an old one, and your boots, shoes, slippers, etc., will last a great deal longer.

A pair of well-made shoes is recognized by this sign : when they are placed beside each other, they touch only at the big toe and at the heel. The soles follow the outline in order that the foot may rest at ease the full length.

Care of the Feet.

Wash the feet each day, and use pumice stone to remove all callous spots.

I said that the feet should be washed daily. This must not be confounded with the daily bath.

Walking warms the feet. Foot

warmers and also open fires are not conducive either to beauty or health. They induce varicose troubles in the legs.

When traveling in cold weather, wear high leggings over the shoes to prevent chilblains. Fur-lined carriage shoes are even more comfortable, but are clumsy things to handle. In the country light sabots are indispensable for walking in the garden in damp weather. Sabots, india rubbers, etc., should not be worn in the house. A bath of *tilleul* is a great relief to tired feet.

After long standing, a salt bath is excellent for resting the feet. Put a handful of sea salt in four quarts of water as hot as can be borne. Immerse the feet, and with the hand throw the water on the legs as high as the knee.

When the water cools, dry briskly with a rough towel.

This treatment, repeated night and morning, will cure neuralgia of the feet. When the feet are swollen from a long walk, or standing, it is well to bathe them in water in which wood ashes have been boiled. Before putting the feet in, strain the water through a cloth. Swelling and fatigue disappear rapidly. Alcoholic friction is also advised. If the feet perspire unpleasantly, a good remedy is bathing them with water containing a little borax; afterward, powder the feet with the dust of lycopodium.

The following also may be tried: Salicylic acid, three parts; talc, seven parts; starch, nine parts. Pulverize and mix the three substances. Powder the feet with this preparation,

Sprinkle boric acid on the inside of the shoes.

However, consult a physician before using any of these remedies. I believe that these recipes are harmless; but I also know that it is sometimes dangerous to suppress perspiration. One can at least change the stockings two or three times each day.

Ingrowing Nails.

This is a most painful infirmity. If the nails are cut squarely, and not almond shaped, on both the great toe and small one, they will not grow in.

But when the evil is there, we must try to cure it. Make a soft paste with mutton suet, pure soap, powdered sugar, in equal parts, and apply until the flesh is forced back.

Or, wet the whole foot and dry it

well.   Afterward, apply to the affected part a solution of gutta percha and chloroform.   The operation should be repeated about four times the first day.   The next day the number of applications may be reduced.

The following is the formula : Chloroform, eighty parts ; gutta percha, ten parts.   This most efficacious remedy is due to Dr. Potain.

Another : Loosen the flesh, cut the nail, moisten the affected part with a camel's hair brush soaked in perchlorate of iron.   The flesh is thus made insensible and hard.   This remedy is said to be infallible.

Corns.

This infirmity is, fortunately, not without a remedy, whatever may have caused it.

A shoe which is too large is almost as injurious as one which is too small. The foot which is not properly supported rubs constantly against the leather in moving, and this rubbing produces corns almost as surely as compression.

When the corn is a new formation, it may be removed by the use of pumice stone.

When it is tender, applications of wool, soaked in castor oil, or rose geranium leaves, preserved in oil, are often all that is necessary to cure it.

A poultice made of bread crumbs, soaked in vinegar thirty minutes, will remove a corn in one night.

Good results are obtained from dissolving a false pearl in vinegar; the creamy substance is then applied to the corn. So Cleopatra did not live in vain. The corn should be covered at night with a fine cloth, and care taken to keep it well in place.

Orpin, a topical epithem, may be applied to hard corns, which it softens and makes easy to remove. A raw onion, crushed, has the same virtue, and also the leaf of the ground ivy, soaked in vinegar. Besides this, the leaf serves to protect the corn. A little wet plaster of paris, made into a paste, answers the same purpose, as does also a corn plaster, with a hole in the center. This plaster is made of agaric amadouvier (agaric of the oak), which is applied to the corn and thus protects it from the pressure of the shoe.

The following are more scientific formulæ for preparing ointments for removing corns. They resemble each

other slightly, but these trifling differ-
ences may make them the more suitable for the various kinds of corns :

First. Salicylic acid, four grammes ;
atropine, ten centigrammes ; flexible
collodion, thirty grammes.

Second. Salicylic acid, twenty
grammes ; extract cannabis indica, two
grammes ; collodion, 120 grammes.

Third. Salicylic acid, one gramme ;
extract canabis indica, fifty centigrammes ; alcohol, at 90°, one gramme ;
ether, at 62°, two grammes, fifty centigrammes ; flexible collodion, five
grammes. (Formula of P. Vigier.)

Whichever of these remedies is used,
mix the substances together, and put
them in a well-corked bottle. Saturate
a small camel's hair brush with the mixture, and apply it at least twice to the
corn. Repeat this treatment daily for

two weeks; at the end of this time soak the foot for one hour in warm water.

The bunion, which particularly affects the joint of the big toe, and sometimes the ball of the foot (in which case heels should not be worn on the shoes), is cured in several different ways.

First. If it is inflamed, cover it with a plaster and wear soft slippers. Anoint the affected part with a salve composed of seven and one-half grammes of iodine mixed with thirty grammes of lard.

Second. Cover the bunion with a piece of oiled silk, over an application of animal fat.

Third. Take a piece of doeskin, make a hole in it large enough to receive the bunion, and place it over the inflamed spot. Cover with oiled silk. Over this rub the bunion twice each day with a salve of animal fat and iodine.

Fourth. A plaster of diachylon is excellent. A bunion may also be trimmed and cauterized with sulphate of copper, which is sold in sticks, like nitrate of silver.

Cramps.

Cramps are most distressing.

They are produced by the wearing of shoes too tight across the toes.

It is said that persons subject to cramps at night are immediately relieved by raising the head. This may be done by extra pillows, or by putting two bricks under the castors at the head of the bed.

I can vouch for the truth of the statement that remedies containing arsenic, even in infinitesimal proportions, produce terrible cramps in the calf of the leg.

The Care of Shoes.

Damp shoes should be at once removed on entering the house. If filled with dry oats the grain absorbs the dampness and prevents the leather from hardening. They should never be placed near a fire. Let the oats remain until the following day. When dry, they may be used again in the same way.

Filling the shoes with paper produces the same result; the dampness will be absorbed, and the shoe retain its shape.

Paraffin softens shoes which have been hardened by dampness, and restores their flexibility. Heavy hunting boots are softened by exposure to the smoke of broom straw, or if rubbed with sweet oil and lard. It makes them easier to wear, and they last twice as long, and protect the feet more effectually against damp and cold.

To make the soles of shoes last longer, and render them impervious to water, warm them slightly, and give them coats of copal varnish, drying them after each coat.

A mixture of cream and ink is excellent. The varnish used on harnesses is equally good for preserving kid boots. Take a very small quantity on a bit of cloth and rub it on well. Polish it with a piece of dry cloth.

In orange-growing countries they cut an orange in half, rub the juicy side on the soot of an iron pot, and then into the boot. The boot is then brushed with a soft brush, which gives it a high polish.

To prevent shoes from creaking or cracking, rub the soles with linseed oil, or place them on a plate full of the oil, and they will absorb it. This renders them water and snowproof.

How to Put on Lace or Button Shoes.

The stockings should always be longer than the feet. They must be well pulled at the toes, in order that the heel may find its proper place.

Very few people know how to button or lace their shoes properly. Generally the lace is pulled too tightly, and the foot often made extremely uncomfortable. Place the heel firmly in the shoe, then move the toes until they feel comfortable. After these preliminaries, put your foot on a chair in front of you, and proceed to lace the shoe over the instep as tightly as possible, but gradually, in order to keep the foot firm in the shoe, while giving the toes perfect liberty. At the ankle the lacing must be done so as to give com-fort to that part of the foot.

The same process is necessary when putting on buttoned boots. Begin with the third button above the vamp, and fasten as far as the ankle; before going farther, return to the first two buttons. Lastly, button that part which covers the leg, doing this as loosely as possible, for pressure there is injurious to health.

MYSTERIES OF THE TOILET.

LINGERIE.

" Make it orderly and well,
According to the fashion and the time."

A TRULY refined woman is instinctive-
ly fastidious about her personal linen.

I have been told that in the days
when bustles were worn, many rich
ladies secured the abnormal size, which
filled all artists with despair, by the use
of worn-out muffs, old lingerie rolled
up, and other articles of that kind.

On the other hand, shop girls econo-
mized on their underclothing, in order
to buy wire or hair bustles, which they
were obliged to renew as fast as they
lost their shape.

Dressmakers say that society women

do not hesitate to send them, as models, bodices with linings shockingly soiled, which have never been properly cared for. I have seen superb gowns worn over frayed satin skirts covered with mud.

Undergarments may be simple, but they should be as irreproachable as the gown itself.

They should be cut as gracefully as possible. If they can be made of fine materials so much the better, but rather than to own them in limited number, insufficient for daily changes, it is preferable to purchase less costly ones, and so secure the necessary number.

Underwear of surah and colored batiste has somewhat lost favor recently. Many refined women have always clung to the use of fine white linen, or even cotton, which may be easily washed either at home, or by a good laundress, and which are returned to the wardrobe smelling sweetly.

Chemises of colored surah, rose, blue, mauve, etc., have, according to my taste, this drawback, that they can never be subjected to a thorough washing. For this reason, they are of doubtful elegance. Well-bred women object to the over-elaborate trimming of under-garments. They prefer a moderate use of laces, which must always be *real*, which are not injured by washing. What can be more agreeable than to put on fresh lingerie?

Black stockings are now but little worn, except for the street. With the slippers and low shoes which fashion now decrees for the house, silk hose of the same color must be worn.

Corsets and Their Detractors.

The corset has many detractors.

Some say that it destroys the form of a woman, others, that it ruins her health.

"Look at the statues of antiquity," they cry, "those *chefs-d'œuvres*, which represent the real beauty of the human body as it came from the hand of Nature.   Have the Venuses small waists like the modern women ?   No, no, this divine structure has not been confined, put under restraint, it has been freely developed, has blossomed out.   Such a goddess may bear children, and transmit to her son strength and health."

Charles X., who remembered the long wasp-waisted corset of Marie Antoinette, was a savage enemy of the corset.

One of my scientific friends assures me that the corset has so flattened the ribs, which in a healthy woman should be curved, that the feminine skeleton of to-day will puzzle scientists in the ages to come.

The Genevese physician, Tronchin, attributed the greater part of the feminine diseases of his day to corsets, and to mitigate the evil he says he induced the women to adopt the Watteau gown, under which they could loosen the horrible instrument of torture.

How many husbands have quoted to their wives the example of Mme. Tallien, who disdained, all her life long, to imprison her pretty figure in whalebone and satin, and who for all that, perhaps on account of that, was considered the most attractive woman of her day.

Advantages of the Corset.

The detractors of the corset are right when they blame the foolish women who deform their bodies and destroy their health to reduce the size of the waist half an inch, an infinitesimal advantage, especially when one thinks of the price paid : compression of the vital organs, difficulty in breathing, congestion of the face. (There are women who go so far that they imperil the function of maternity.)

But if the corset is only worn as a support for the frail bust, it becomes, on the contrary, useful. Elasticity and flexibility have been given to it, and this insures perfect comfort and ease, which means graceful movements. The waist is supple, bends like a reed in the wind, and does not offend us by a rigidity which reminds one of the steel armor worn by the knights of old.

Corsets are absolutely essential to stout women. They restrain the excess of flesh, and without them it is impossible to make a stout woman look trim. However expensive her garments, she would not appear well dressed, and would always look slovenly.

The corset supports the skirts, which would otherwise hang too heavily upon the waist; without its assistance a thin or slender woman could not carry herself well. At the least movement she would appear hipshot. The corset has also another good quality: it serves as a support to the breast, whose distended fibers would soon relax and fall too low if this restraint

did not keep it in its place, and so
preserve it in that form which "serves
as a model for the cup on the altar."

How the Corset should be Made.

The corset should have bones only
in the back and front, unless the
person for whom it is made has lost
her true proportions; in that case it
should be supported on the sides also.

Coutil   is   too   stiff   a   material,
according to my opinion, for corsets.
Satin, even cotton satin, is preferable,
since we do not need armor; but the
best of all materials for women who
are not too stout is doeskin.

We shall, doubtless, reach this point
of perfection, for we already have open
lace corsets for summer use, and corsets which are enlarged at will, thanks
to the elastics with which they are pro-

vided.   These are intended for feeble
and delicate women.

A short corset is, in every respect,
preferable to a long one, since comfort
and grace are at stake.   If the corset
is too high under the arms it makes
the shoulders high, which is not desirable.   If too long, it lengthens the
waist unbecomingly, and the legs seem
too short, and thus the happy harmony
which constitutes true beauty is destroyed.   The corset which is short on
the hips leaves the movements free.
Do not be indifferent to the shape of
the corset.

The shorter the corset the smaller
the waist.   Large, stiff corsets give a
wooden appearance, and increase the
size of the waist.

Do not allow fashion to rule you,
when it decides in favor of those

sheaths which give one the appearance
of an automaton.   Resist with all
your strength the dressmaker who insists upon putting you into one.   If
you have allowed yourself to be im-
prisoned in the stiff cuirass, unlace the
top holes and the two lower ones, and
let the middle ones be so laced as not
to press you at all.   Thanks to this
artifice, you may really be comfortable
in this corset until you get another.

A corset should always be perfectly
fresh.   A soiled one indicates a careless wearer.   It should be protected
by a corset cover, and washed as soon
as soiled.   Whatever be the material
of which it is made, whatever its color,
white, blue, pink, or mauve, never
wear it after it loses its freshness.   The
gray, or mastic colored corset always
looks soiled.

It cannot be denied that the black corset is economical. It has the advantage of not soiling, for it is perfectly easy to preserve its white lining clean until worn out. A black corset in good condition is certainly to be preferred to a soiled white one.

The Leg.

When a child's legs have a tendency to curve, do not let it walk. Let it roll on a carpet, where it can twist and turn at its ease, and the little legs will soon straighten themselves.

In order to avoid varicose troubles, women should avoid fastening their garters too tightly. Exercise develops the leg and enlarges the calf. Excepting for the fact that high gaiters make the leg appear unshapely, they are excellent when walking.

Garters.

Garters are an article of the toilet which should be carefully considered. They may be very simple, or fastened with a jeweled buckle; they must be irreproachable. They should always be clean and fresh, never ragged or threadbare.

I do not admire garters trimmed with laces or ornamented with flowers. In America they are worn of different colors; one pair is composed of one yellow and one black garter, or of one yellow and one blue garter, etc. One of the garters *must* be yellow, as this is said to bring good luck. I do not know whether the yellow is to be worn on the right or left leg. This dissimilarity is very ugly, and one must have a great deal of faith in the talismanic virtue of the yellow garter to willfully commit such a crime against good taste. Common, cheap garters are neither durable nor elegant.*

Securing the Stocking.

Many women endure the pressure of a garter sufficiently tight to hold the stocking. When the circulation is impeded the legs swell, and varicose veins are sometimes formed. In this case the stockings may be fastened to the corset by tapes. But accidents may happen; what if the stretched tapes, which keep the stocking from wrinkling, should give way? Down go the

---

* Whenever an Englishman or Frenchman wishes to account for an *outré* fashion he solemnly adds it to the list of American outrages. I think I am correct in saying the wearing of the one yellow garter originated in Paris, and that the dubious fashion was introduced by an Opera Bouffe so-called *artiste.*—H. H. A.

stockings to the heels. What a state of affairs! I advise wearing a garter not too tight, but sufficiently so to hold up the stocking in case of an accident.

The garter should not be worn below the knee, for this is absolutely contrary to the laws of æsthetics. The form of the calf is injured, and the natural line of beauty destroyed.

Besides, one no longer sees any women, except perhaps old peasants, who tie the garter below the knee, and this is made necessary by the short stockings they wear.

All women who wear long stockings have for many years worn the garter above the knee. It is only in the distant provinces that the fashion of tying them with tape, listing, sometimes with twine, still exists. The

most humble servant wears elastic garters fastened with a buckle ; before ten
years let us hope that the garters we
condemn will have entirely disappeared.

The Chemise.

The chemise, the short underskirt,
the corset cover, should match if possible, and be made of fine percale or
batiste, trimmed with embroidery or
lace. The prettiest chemise is cut heart-
shaped ; a ribbon passed through a
casing or narrow insertion keeps it close
to the neck. It may also be fastened
on the shoulder by a bow of ribbon,
and the neck and arm holes bordered
with a lace edge or narrow embroidery.

The chemise should not be too volu-
minous or too long. The underskirts
should be of taffeta silk corresponding
in color with the gown. White muslin

or percale petticoats are no longer considered good form for the street, and
embroidered and lace trimmed skirts,
except for the house, are tabooed.

The Nightdress.

The flannel or underclothing worn
during the day should never be worn at
night. This is unhealthy as well as uncleanly. The nightdress should fall to
the feet, have sleeves to the elbow or
wrist, and may be trimmed with embroidery or lace. It may be finished
with a high collarette falling in plaits
to the shoulder ; fastened with ribbons
at the neck and wrists. It should be
made of material which will stand washing.

After taking off the night clothes, if
they are not changed each day, they
should be allowed to air for several

hours. Delicately bred women, however, never wear any garment which comes in contact with the skin but once before it is washed. The lingerie may be as simple as possible—to suit the fastidious it must be of exquisitely fine material, and never have come in contact with a sewing-machine.

Early Morning Toilet.

I have said that it was better to wash the face with hot water and soap at night, in order not to expose the skin to the air immediately after being washed.* In the morning bathe the

* Many women declare they cannot wash their faces with soap because it makes them so tender. I insist that the face cannot be kept *clean* without soap. The trouble is generally that the soap is not thoroughly washed *out* of the skin—and in consequence irritates it. If the soap is *pure*, and the face thoroughly rinsed, it will not make the most delicate skin sore. When we discover a method of keeping our *hands* perfectly clean without soap, it will be safe to adopt it for our faces.—H. H. A.

face in warm water, dry with a fine
towel, then take a full bath, followed by
brisk rubbing, or, if this is impossible
daily, a thorough sponge bath is indispensable. Time and trouble are well
repaid by the wholesome results.
Women who go out immediately after
breakfast should dress the hair for the
day on rising.

Women who attend to household
duties should make a second toilet
later in the day, carefully removing all
traces of dust from face, neck, and hair.

The woman who does her own work,
as well as the one who simply superin-
tends the house, should, when she arises,
put on clothing that is clean, spotless,
without rents, and as becoming as
possible. Change the undergarments,
stockings, skirts, etc., as well as the
gown, when the toilet is made in the

afternoon, whether one goes out or remains at home.

The Night Toilet.

Many persons prefer to take a bath at night. In any case it is indispensable either at night or in the morning, and most refreshing. Brush the hair at night, in order to remove the dust which may have gathered during the day. For its arrangement at this hour instructions are given in the chapter on hair.

Removal of Garments.

Never put away immediately in drawers or wardrobe any articles which have just been taken off. Hang them in a place which the air reaches for at least an hour. Put them away after having brushed and folded them.

Clothing which is not laundried should be hung out to air during the day, from time to time, turned wrong side out.

Clothing which has been worn a long time, if not aired properly, contracts most disagreeable odors, and no perfume will conceal them.

Air, water, sunshine, and fire have disinfecting qualities which are purifying; and we should know how to avail ourselves of them.

PART THIRD.

PART THIRD.

ADVICE AND RECIPES.

" *You should be ruled and led by some discretion.*"

Alimentation.

To avoid old age, that bankruptcy of women, take enough nourishment, varied according to the season. An early breakfast of milk is excellent. Eat little at the second. breakfast, es-pecially if there is any work to be done. The principal repast of the Roman soldiers and workmen was taken at night, after the daily labors were over. At the second breakfast an egg and one vegetable are sufficient. Dine at six o'clock—seven at the latest; do not have too many courses. Take a little cup of milk and a light biscuit on going to bed. A diet which is too succulent, too dainty, the abuse of strong meats, condiments, spices, liquors, and rich wine, are enemies of the complexion.

To secure and retain a fine color, partake sparingly of animal food. Meat once a day, and in moderate quantities, is sufficient. Vegetables, on the contrary, may be used more abundantly. Some are more favorable to beauty than others. In the fourteenth and fifteenth centuries they made soups à *la* Morgeline (white chickweed), in order to freshen the complexion. These soups were called "soupes au roi," because Odette de Champdivers, who nursed Charles VI., first administered this herb to him as a remedy. White chickweed was also eaten as a salad. Decoctions and infusions were also made from it to relieve the face of eruptions.

Chickweed should resume the place given it, then, since as a food it has retained all its virtues.

A rhyming proverb of the Renaissance recommends especially certain vegetables :

> Through spinach and leek,
> Lily tints in a week.

To these may be added the cucumber, carrot, tomato, and all other good vegetables. Graham and rye bread should have a prominent place among the selected articles of food. A slice of either between the second breakfast and dinner will not injure the stomach. Too much butter, lard, grease, and oil should not be used in cooking, as they are injurious to the complexion. Pastry should only be eaten about once a week, and sugar should be used sparingly. Bonbons almost never; acids not at all. Conserves should not be eaten daily. In many cases cheese is excluded, except Gruyère, which is wholesome. Tea, coffee, and chocolate are not injurious, provided they are used in moderation. Milk and lemonade are, on the contrary, excellent for the complexion. Wine should be weakened : with at least double the quantity of well filtered water.

Boire de l'eau
Fait le teint beau,
Boire du vin
Fait le gros teint.

A glass of hot water before dinner improves the complexion. It is a good plan to weaken wine with mineral and digestive waters.

Fruit should always be eaten after meals. Eat strawberries freely in their season, if you have no tendency to eczema; they cool the blood and the liver, and are said to cure gout and rheumatism, if aided by a strict diet. The cherry has the same qualities. It is prescribed also for vesania, a disease of the mind. The red raspberry is very refreshing; so is the plum. The peach (the rose among fruits) is very good for the stomach.

The apple is the most wholesome of all fruit. Its good qualities are innumerable. The orange may also be recommended highly.

It is asserted the Baroness X., who was one of the beauties at the court of Louis Philippe, and who at eighty-four years of age still had brilliant eyes and the fresh skin of a girl, lived entirely on oranges for forty years. One dozen for her breakfast, one dozen at noon, one dozen and a slice of bread and glass of Bordeaux for her dinner.

I advise no one to put themselves on this diet, but it is certain that the most beautiful women are, generally, as temperate as camels. The Marquise de Crequy, who lived during the last century, and died when almost a hundred, for fifty years ate only vegetables cooked in chicken broth and grilled compôtes. She drank nothing but water, except during her pregnancy, when her physicians required her to take sweetened wine. During the last forty years of her life a little candied sugar was put in the water which she drank. Several women of my acquaintance, who have perfect complexions, live upon vegetables and cooked fruits, and drink only water during the Lenten season.

Some women follow the forty days' abstinence imposed by the Church, with two extra weeks of fruit and vegetable diet. They give as a reason for this penance the necessity of destroying the effects of fish, which is eaten so largely during Lent, and which is apt to produce pimples on the purest skins. On this account many women

very seldom eat sea food, and especially avoid shell fish.

If the advice here given is followed,
the results obtained will be surprising.
Diet does much more for the complexion than physicians and drugs.

Beauty is impossible without health.
As soon as one feels indisposed, a
strict diet of short or longer duration,
is generally the best remedy. By this
we mean abstaining from rich dishes
and heavy wines ; the hours of meals
should be arranged at equal intervals.

Recollect always that what serves to
sustain life may also destroy it. To
keep in good health be careful to place
some limit on the appetite.

In the spring especially the diet is of
the greatest importance. A celebrated
physician told me that the medicinal

spring time should begin the last of January.

As age draws on, the quantity of nourishment should be diminished, and only articles of food which are digest-ible selected. After sixty this be-comes imperative.

The Life One Should Lead.

A charming old lady revealed the secret of her fair and rosy complexion to a group of young women as follows: "Late hours," said she, "and over-sleeping ruin the complexion. Go to bed early, arise early, and you will grow old slowly, and retain your good looks to an advanced age. If, how-ever, your position forces you into so-ciety and you are obliged to be up late at night, sleep an hour every after-noon. Before going to bed take a hot bath and remain in the water only a few moments. Then drink a cup of bouillon, and a small glass of Malaga wine. Sleep will soon follow, and last until the natural time of awakening, which is about ten o'clock in the morning under these circumstances. Take a cold plunge or sponge bath, a light breakfast of *café au lait*, and bread without any butter." The old lady added: "See how necessary it is to give as little of ourselves as possible to society, and how much precious time (never to be regained) we waste in fêtes and pleasures."

She continued: "Out-of-door exercise is an absolute necessity, but must not be carried to excess. A daily walk is excellent, and it is scarcely necessary to say that whole days of lawn tennis, croquet, etc., are not favorable to the complexion."

Wear warm, light garments, to secure an even temperature. In winter it is even more important to protect the spine than the chest. Wear a silk sleeveless jacket next the skin, if you do not wish to wear a flannel one. At any rate, if you are delicate, young or old, cover, the spine with a strip of flannel tied by a ribbon, and extending to the hips. There will be no need to fear colds, bronchitis, phthisis, if this precaution is taken, and it does not prevent wearing a decolletté gown.

Never wear tight clothing. It is injurious to health and beauty. The face becomes congested when the organs are compressed, the hands swell, and get red, and the carriage awkward. Wear easy corsets, gloves, and shoes.

Take, from time to time, in the

morning, a glass of some saline water, If the complexion is muddy, take a tea-spoonful of powdered charcoal, mixed with honey, on going to bed, three nights in succession. Follow this by a light purgative.

All forms of iron and Peruvian bark have a ruinous effect upon the complexion. Alkaline solutions, mixed with a slight quantity of arsenic, on the contrary, are very beneficial.* When in good health, sponge the body each day with cold water. Live in a wholesome house. In winter do not allow the temperature to fall below 53° Fahrenheit in the bedrooms. Work; keep yourself busy, read, take an interest in the great and beautiful things of Nature and Humanity.

* Arsenic should not be taken under any circumstances except by advice of a physician.—K. H. A.

Activity of the body and spirit delays old age. Avoid excitements and senseless luxury, and do not allow yourself to be governed by violent emotions.

A sober life refines the features. Gluttony materializes and deforms the body. Temperance in all things will preserve beauty and freshness of complexion.

Do not paint your face in youth if you wish to preserve your complexion in old age. When threads of silver begin to sprinkle your hair, do not have recourse to dyes, which cause it to fall out, and destroy its glossiness, fineness, and elasticity. Beautiful white hair makes a far more becoming frame for the face in old age than bands of raven black hair or blond curls.

Do not keep too many odorous

flowers around. " Flowers," said an old physician to one of my very pretty aunts, "are jealous of a woman's beauty, and try to destroy it." This was a gallant metaphor, which was intended to convince his beautiful patients of the danger that existed in having too many flowers about one. The headaches which frequently follow certainly do not beautify.

Gymnastic exercises have been highly recommended for middle-aged women. When it is necessary to use the arms, why not exercise them on housework? This advice was recently given to a northern queen, who followed it, and profited thereby. With hands covered with gloves one can dust, brush, or sweep, as necessity requires. This gymnastic exercise is sufficient and useful, natural and wholesome, and one does not appear ridiculous while engaged in it.

All the members of the body should be exercised. Cultivate a cheerful disposition. As we advance in life, let us become more indulgent and kind. A kind nature and calmness of mind are among the indispensable conditions for retaining beauty.

In old age, let us not attempt to look too young. A dowager in a low-necked tulle gown, with her head adorned with flowers, is grotesque. She should wear rich and heavy materials, cover her hair with a fichu of lace, and drape a scarf about her aged shoulders.

An old woman dressed like a young girl is something terrible to look at. We may still love youth—in others— and should always greet it with pleasant smiles.

In one word, let us accept the inevitable gracefully. One must grow old, but with care we may still remain charming, and be beloved by our children, and our friends of all ages.

Secrets of Beauty.

In the care of the skin consider carefully its texture. Dry and oily skins, flaccid and firm ones require very different treatment.

But whatever happens, beware of charlatans, and only use the preparations of well-known manufacturers, whose merits are attested by physicians. Bathe in river, spring, or rain water, if possible. The juice of melons, of cucumber, slightly oily, is good for dry skins. The juice of strawberries will thoroughly cleanse an oily skin. An infusion of flowers of lavender or of marjolan (origan) is a tonic, and will harden the flesh.

These remedies must not be abused, and never be used daily. All treatment should be interrupted from time to time, and for several days. Any remedy loses its effect as soon as the body becomes accustomed to it.

A faded face (dry skins always fade soonest) may be freshened by the use of a wash which we here give.

Boil the soft part of bread and marshmallow roots in filtered rain water. When the water has evaporated a little pass a bag of lye through it, then add the yellow of eggs (in strong proportion) and fresh cream. Mix well, and perfume with orange-flower water.*

This water is unfit to use after standing, so it must be prepared afresh each

* This recipe is too indefinite to be indorsed.—H. H. A.

time.   Plantain water is equally well recommended.

Pretty Octogenarians.

An octogenarian, we have already remarked, may still be beautiful and charming.   I have seen more than one example of this persistence of beauty at an advanced age.   At eighty-five, the Maréchale Davout, Princesse d'Eckmühl, the wife of the conqueror of d'Auerstädt, still had the carriage of a queen, superb eyes, and the finest complexion in the world, so white as to rival her snowy hair.

She never used anything but rain water for washing her face.   Her table was simply served, excepting on the days when she entertained, and even then she did not depart from her abstemiousness.   She was generous, kind-hearted,

and gracious, a truly *grande dame*, preserving until the last her charm and
grace.   Although one of the most beautiful women of her day, she cared little
for the triumphs of beauty.   She was
always constant to the one love of her
life, her soldier husband, and her
thoughts were ever with him, and the
dangers he was exposed to.   Old age
neither frightened nor saddened this
brave spirit, and although she endured
great sorrow she daily grew more attractive.   Her eyes reflected only
wholesome thoughts, and she was sur-
rounded by that halo which encircles
the heads of strong, virtuous women.
Everyone has heard of her daughter,
the Marquise de Blocqueville, mistress
of the most delightful house in Paris,
whose literary talent alone places her
in the first ranks ; possessing kindness,

generosity, and exquisite grace, finding her happiness in giving joy to others, making everyone appear at his best, her pure brow reflects her noble thoughts. Like her mother, she has white hair, which she lightly powders, and which adds to the resemblance she bears to the adorable women of the eighteenth century. The marquise dresses with rare elegance, without, however, spending as much money on her toilets as other women of her rank. Coquetry to woman is a duty, even to the end.

In her charming book of thoughts, so poetically called Chrysanthemums, the marquise says: "Coquetry, in old age, is a holy coquetry, for it bids us take greater care not to *displease* than youth takes to *please*."

All elderly women would do well to

copy the toilet of Madame de Blocqueville, instead of taking their grand-
daughters as models.

"The time will come," said the marquise, "when each woman will dress
according to her own style, regardless
of prevailing modes."

These are the secrets of remaining
beautiful, and of pleasing to the end.

OBESITY AND LEANNESS.

"'Twixt two extremes, the golden mean."

EXCESSIVE flesh deforms the human body, and causes it to lose all grace. A woman sees herself growing stout with terror, for then she must bid adieu to the ideally beautiful line of her profile, the delicate outlines of her bust, the gracefulness of her figure.

There are women who have the courage to follow the severest of treatments to save their beauty, and they do well, for it is a woman's duty not only to acquire beauty, but to retain it.

One day the Empress Elizabeth of Austria perceived that her beautifully

modeled chin was losing its curve of
outline, and her waist growing larger.
She was horrified. Must she lose that
slenderness which made her appear
twenty years younger than she really
was, that proud carriage of a goddess?
No, no; she would do anything to
remain the most beautiful sovereign
of Europe, and she, the finest horse-
woman in the world, renounced riding,
and took long walks every day, and in
all kinds of weather.

A little later on Queen Marguerite
of Italy was threatened with too much
embonpoint. She also was unwilling to
lose her reputation as a pretty woman,
so she grasped the alpenstock of the
tourist, and scaled the highest moun-
tains in her kingdom.

Before these, Diane de Poitiers
walked each day, "In order to retain
her beauty."

A woman who is too stout cannot take a step without blowing like a grampus, without perspiring in torrents ; she is as clumsy as an elephant ; her figure grows thick, her hips become enormous, making her look vulgar, whatever may be her naturally distinguished appearance. Her cheeks and her eyelids, overcharged with fat, make a repulsive mass of her face. She loses beauty, form, grace.

I would not paint this portrait, I would not dissect the ugliness inflicted by obesity, if I did not wish to awaken coquetry in women who have allowed themselves to grow unwieldy, and if I did not know that the evil could be remedied by courage and will.

I have merely held up a mirror, before performing the offices of a physician, and, if I have been cruel, it was to impress the supreme importance of seeking a cure which is within the reach of all.

How to Avoid Obesity.

Obesity might often be avoided if people did not yield to laziness, if the mind were kept engaged, if the body were exercised, if ease were less sought after, long slumbers in eider down and resting in easy-chairs avoided. Has a stout peasant ever been seen?

It is necessary, when there is a tendency to obesity, to live with almost Spartan frugality. But the evil of gluttony is sometimes stronger than the love of coquetry and the desire to enjoy good health. And yet the poor, who never dine with Lucullus, are seldom disfigured with surplus fat.

Come, then, unfortunate victims of obesity, bestir yourselves. Work until the perspiration bedews your brow.

Be of use in the world. No one has the right to be idle.

Reduce your table. Give up your rich food and fattening wines. Suppress one dish to-day, another to-morrow. Spend the money these unnecessary luxuries would cost on some poor neighbor. You will be doing a charity to two persons, yourself and some unfortunate who counts his crusts of bread.

Take this for your motto : "Work and frugality," and thus you will save yourself.

How to Grow Thin.

Physical exercise is recognized as one of the great remedies for bringing the body back to its just proportions. It quickens the respiration and increases the quantity of oxygen taken

into the lungs. Oxygen consumes
carbon, which is thus prevented from
being converted into fat. You need
not, therefore, fear fatigue, and should
arise early in the morning and keep
about all day ; walk, ride ; rest only at
night. Never lie down during the day.

Exercise must be accompanied by
extreme temperance and a strict diet ;
that is to say, take no nourishment
which tends to produce fat, especially
farinaceous foods (wheat, rye, oatmeal,
rice, Irish potatoes, sago, etc.), which
rapidly increase flesh. Compare the
pullet in its coop with the carnivor-
ous animal. The enforced inactivity
of the one results in layers of fat
on its body ; while the other, left in
a savage state, knows no idleness or
excesses in eating, and consequently
never grows fat.

Let those who are beginning to grow too stout listen to my cry of warning. Renounce the confectioner, give up pastries and all sweets. Even bread and vegetables must be doled out to you sparingly.

You may eat moderately underdone meats, eggs, green vegetables, salads, mushrooms, fruits, etc. Control your appetite as much as possible.

Drink but little while eating, and weaken your wine with vichy or apollinaris, which have the property of expelling the gases from the body. While dieting is necessary and to be commended, I cannot too strongly condemn many of the anti-fat nostrums and so-called reduction pills. They are drastic compounds and powerful purgatives, and should never be taken except by a physician's orders. In many cases they so reduce the patient as to induce heart-failure. And the loss of flesh is but temporary ; the moment the powerful medicine is withdrawn the flesh returns.

Discard the idea that coffee will make one thin. On the contrary, it has a tendency to fatten. It is not the quantity of nutritive matter which it contains which produces this result, but its digestive properties. It facilitates digestion so well, makes it so complete, that not one of the nourishing particles escapes assimilation. All that can nourish and fatten is absorbed under the influence of this powerful stimulant. Tea has the same effect, but in a lesser degree.

Obesity is an enemy to the strength of man and the beauty of woman. It impedes the respiration, and makes moving about difficult : diminishes the strength of the muscles, the energies of the nerves, and destroys all suppleness and activity.

The most attractive form, the most refined face, becomes heavy and uninteresting as the outlines of the features are lost in this superfluity of fat. As the body becomes overgrown it loses that harmony which nature has given to this quasi-divine structure of man.

Lastly, obesity predisposes to apoplexy and dropsy. "Full bodies are more subject to sudden death," said Hippocrates, "than thin ones." Stout people rarely attain to a ripe old age.

Thin Women.

Angular lines, and the absence of flesh, which allows the bones to protrude, are misfortunes to women, and besides this, thinness is almost always accompanied by a bad complexion.

Listen to the jests which are made concerning thin women: " She is thin as a rail." " She is as flat as a shingle."

It is a mistake to think, as some poor dried-up women do, that one must be thin to be distinguished looking.

Thinness is sometimes the result of an acrid, disagreeable character. I mention this because it may be corrected. The nervous, fretful woman, who not only torments herself, but others ; who is excitable, impatient, and restless, is sure to lose all feminine grace.

Excitability must not be confounded with healthful activity, which is advantageous to beauty, health, and a well ordered life.

A thin woman has usually a complexion like lead, or a muddy skin, because, as is commonly but justly said, "She makes bad blood." (*Elle se fait du mauvais sang.*)

But if she chooses she may become fair, rosy, and well rounded.

Means for Acquiring Flesh.

Thinness is often caused by badly selected, insufficient nourishment; or by fatigue, either physical or mental, or by nervous and bilious temperament, a melancholy disposition. "Remember that bones and a sweet temper never dwell under the same roof."

"Laugh and grow fat." Retire early, rise late, but always at a regular hour. Take moderate exercise, when the weather permits. Have your meals served each day at the same hours

Eat good food, abundantly, but never to excess. It should be composed principally of farinaceous substances, of good quality, easily digested and assimilated. The most important are bread, soups, tapioca, sago, oatmeal gruel* and rice.

Meat must occupy a secondary place in this diet, and must be of good quality. The early breakfast should be composed of *café au lait* or chocolate; at the second breakfast take a glass of old Bordeaux, and a cup of black coffee after dinner. Good form and good digestion alike forbid the use of cream or milk in after-dinner coffee. Life must be as calm and devoid of excitement as possible, and pleasure found at home. Take frequent warm

---

* Too much oatmeal is apt to make the complexion coarse.—II. II. A.

baths. Above all, cultivate mildness and sweet temper.

Thus extreme thinness may be remedied. A slender woman, who has a graceful figure, may be attractive; a thin woman is never beautiful. A proverb of Arden says : " Beautiful skin is not found on bones."

Concerning Æsthetics.

One must be a pretty and agreeable woman as well as a good wife and mother to keep the husband and father fond of his home. It is often possible to become pretty and agreeable by taking a little pains. Choose for the toilet colors which harmonize with the skin and hair, and wear well fitting boots and gloves, also pretty home gowns, with sleeves arranged to show to advantage the white and rounded arm.

Indicate the slender waist by a sash, instead of wearing formless garments. Dress the hair so that it will make a becoming frame for the pretty face.

Instead of this, what does one frequently see? Many good women who adore their husbands and earnestly desire to please them, are most careless about their dress, choosing often dull and unbecoming colors for their gowns, and even wearing coarse and ugly shoes. They cover their pretty forms with ill-shaped garments, and sometimes even appear in wrappers in which the body appears of one size from the throat to the feet. It is quite possible for a woman to be what is termed *neatly* and yet most unbecomingly dressed.

Rational Coquetry.

I insist that a certain amount of coquetry is not only allowable, but a duty to our husbands. They will love us better, more ardently, and longer. Is it not worth the trouble? If we lay aside our armor, however pleasant we may make home for them, they are liable to be lured away by cleverer women. They may perhaps remain faithful to us, we may still possess their respect, but they will cling to us from a sense of duty. Duty and pleasure should go hand in hand, and we should allow no other woman to be more charming than ourselves. Many women may be more beautiful than the wife, but if the latter knows how to profit by her natural gifts, and adds to this the proper care of

her person and her toilet, her husband
will never perceive the charms of
others.

Any blemish of the skin which can
be remedied should receive immediate
attention.   It will not do to neglect
this important matter for one moment.
Venus herself would be repulsive with
à spotted, blotchy skin.   Your own
happiness and that of your family may
depend upon it.   When I see a woman
looking slovenly at home, dressed in a
faded and unbecoming gown, I pro-
phesy trouble for the future, spite of
present happiness.   All the feminine
graces should be cultivated for him
whom we adore, and for him we should
try to make ourselves beautiful and
charming.   Do not neglect a daily
walk in the fresh air.   Without this
wholesome exercise it is impossible to

retain health and beauty. Use your intelligence to remain pretty or to become so. Add physical to moral and intellectual culture. Superintend your house and busy yourself with your children. This activity of the body, the heart, and the mind, is necessary to those who desire to remain beautiful and beloved.

Remember that the advice given in this book is offered in the hope of aiding you in being happy; therefore do not despise it.

The Art of Growing Old Gracefully.

" Beauty doth varnish age as if new born,
And gives the crutch the cradle's infancy."

The way to ward off old age is not to fear it, not to allow one's self to be crushed by the dread of advancing years.

Use only legitimate preventatives, and avoid trying experiments with preparations not endorsed by physicians.

Relinquish too youthful toilets, as they but add years to the appearance. Keep up your interest in the young, and do not envy them. Retire with dignity from the struggle, and never pose as a rival to your own daughters. In this way surround your life with sweet, true affections, which prevent the heart from growing bitter.

Do not lose interest in the stirring events of the day, great discoveries, wonderful inventions; do not fall behind the times, and do not harp upon other and better days.

To those who come to you for advice be kind and sympathetic.

As you advance in years, preserve still more carefully your personal ap-

pearance, for if you neglect yourself
ever so slightly the result will be
more disastrous than if you were
younger.

Last of all, your costume should be
one of great simplicity, unpretentious,
yet graceful.

I assure you that under these conditions you may struggle successfully
against old age.

You will still give pleasure to those
about you, " and keep eternal springtime in thy face."

Society Women.

Have you never heard of the Princess Z. and the Duchess X., the Marquise d'Y., etc., etc., of Mme. A., Mme.
B., Mme. C., as young women, who are
beautiful and attractive?

Suddenly you learn that they are

fifty, sixty years old, but you refuse, as do also those who praise and admire them, to admit that they can have reached the age ascribed to them.

These society women, whose only ambition is worldly success and triumph, have determined to remain young and beautiful, and they have succeeded up to a certain point, appearing to be fifteen years younger than the records show.

Not for one moment have they neglected the cultivation of their beauty, and, with an energy worthy of a better cause, have endured all things in order to fight off the approach of old age, to preserve their physical charms intact, and to obtain those which can be secured by pains and study.

They have bravely struggled against

the enemies time has brought : illness, sorrow, or fatigue.

Crushed for one moment, they have arisen, they have struggled, for to them this was a question of life or death. From a society standpoint it has re- solved itself into the query of " to be or not to be."

They have succeeded in conquering Time and Nature.

Without imitating them too closely, which is not always compatible with the life led by an honest and conscientious mother of a family, it is not only proper, but your duty to use all lawful means to stop the onward march of old age and ugliness. This will be easier for you than for the butterflies of fashion. The wholesome activity in which your days are spent is favorable to you, whereas worldly people are constantly

obliged to repair the exhausting fatigues of their lives of pleasure and
restlessness.

They have sought the satisfaction of
self-love and of vanity. Your object
has been to remain the fairy of the
hearthstone, the joy of him to whom
you have devoted your existence.

Art of Appearing always Young.

As a charming old lady once said,
"To remain always young one must
be always amiable."

A melancholy face, a sullen, an evil
look, is like coming in contact with
winter; whereas a serene face, a gracious air, a kind and good expression,
is like a spring day, and a smile on the
lips like its sunshine.

Sulky people, you may have remarked, always appear to be ten years

older than they really are. The face grows wrinkled from contracting the brows; the mouth projects disagreeably when sulking.

Behold beside the portrait of the sullen woman the picture of a sweet and gracious woman : all her features are in repose, her lips form an adorable Cupid's bow, kindness softens her glance, and goodness illuminates her brow.

Perhaps she is the elder, but she will always appear young and charming.

Grace of Movement.

To be graceful, harmony must govern our movements.

The planets move harmoniously; were they to break the law of number and harmony, frightful discord would

be the result in the universe. Disso-
nance destroys harmony in music and
is painful to the ear. It would be easy
to mutiply examples to prove that harmony governs, or should govern all
things, from the march of the stars
down to the gestures of the lowest
form of human life. There are
women who possess in a superior degree the intuition of harmony. I
know some who select unconsciously
their seats, their poses, according to
the toilets which they wear. Dressed
in a simple costume they lean against
a piece of furniture of severe style, or
sit erect upon an oaken chair, which is
in perfect harmony with the appearance they present in their tailor-
made gowns. In the evening, robed
in silks and laces, they as naturally select luxurious sofas, ottomans, and

easy-chairs, which are in perfect accord with their costumes.

This is not possible for the stiff, angular woman, whose movements are brusque and awkward.

Those who know how to walk and carry themselves possess equilibrium. Perhaps this gift of nature has never been lost by acquiring bad habits, or they have re-conquered it by means of study. This is the case with great actresses. Look at them as they walk on to the stage ; at the same time that the feet move, their weight is thrown on the hips, and the body is thus left in equilibrium. Whatever movement they make is correct, because they know the law of harmony. When the actress bows, she bends her body and raises it by the same even, gentle movement.

You will never see her stretch her arm out straight, making a horizontal line in the first movement. If her arm is to be extended, this is only attained at the second movement. It is lifted, then stretched out. If it were straightened at the first movement, the woman would look like a jointed doll. We will give a few hints as to how this science of gracefulness can be cultivated, a gracefulness which is not artificial, as might be supposed, for it rests on a natural principle.

How to Walk.

If you are inclined to stoop, walk to and fro with your hands behind your back when you are alone in the garden, or in your apartment.

Children should be taught to throw

their shoulders back, by being made to walk with elbows close to the body. This will naturally keep the chin free, and the chest thrown forward. The back will curve in ; the shoulder blades be kept in their places instead of projecting ; the bust will arch itself; and the entire weight of the body be thrown on the hips, which is necessary for a perfect equilibrium.

One should practice touching the ground first with the ball of the foot, to avoid walking on the heels with toes in the air, which is ugly, clumsy and ungraceful, exposing the whole system to the useless jolting Nature tried to spare us when she formed the ball of the foot.

When mounting a stairway or climbing a hill, for the sake of the lungs as well as to obtain a graceful carriage, both back and head should be held erect.

Women who have learned how to walk, or who walk naturally, according to these principles, like the goddesses of old, will not crush the flowers on which they tread.

Grace of Form.

To retain your graceful form, then, learn how to carry yourself. If women would be more careful about this while young, they would have finer figures and more slender hips when older. The woman who holds herself straight, who does not draw her chin to the collar of her garment, who keeps back her shoulder blades, and thus rounds out her breast, without an apparent effort keeps her muscles firm and flexible and the desired curve in place of

flatness. Thus the heaviness which is
so much dreaded, and which destroys
all youthfulness and grace, may be
avoided.

The woman who holds herself well,
who throws the weight of her body on
her hips (this cannot be too often repeated) instead of allowing it to be supported by the abdomen, has the carriage
of a queen, the walk of a nymph. Do not
fear that you will acquire a haughty expression. On the contrary, if your
eyes are tender and your smile is amiable, your proud grace will not make
you unsympathetic.

I do not mean by this that you
should carry your head like a vain
peacock, or stiffen yourself, or strut;
but hold the bust in the firm and
straight position which nature de-
signed, whether you walk, or sit, or

stand, so that you may not look like a bundle, but keep your body in its proper position.

By following this advice you will stoop or lean with a thousand times more grace and flexibility than a woman who relaxes, bends, rounds her back from a mere habit of indifference. Nature always punishes us for dis- obedience to her laws. It is her will that the human race should keep the body which she has sculptured erect, with uplifted gaze. If you allow your- self to be drawn down to the earth, you will lose the beauty of your form.

Advice to Stout Women.

A stout woman should not wear a tailor-made suit. It defines the body too distinctly, and accentuates every pound of flesh. She should avoid wearing large bows and rosettes at her belt, either in front or behind ; these ornaments simply increase her size.

She should not wear very short sleeves, as an arm which is fat at the shoulder sometimes unpleasantly reminds one of a ham or a leg of mutton.

A ruche at the neck is not at all becoming to her, nor a high or tight collar. The bodice may be opened slightly at the throat. A feather boa may be worn without disfiguring the wearer.

Short basques exaggerate the size. The hair dressed low is unbecoming to very stout women. It should be worn high on top of the head, without twisting. Bandeaux, if worn, should not be strained, or plastered. Without being untidy, the hair should be loosely dressed, and oils and pomatums should be avoided.

Large figure designs must be excluded from the stout woman's toilet. Striped and plain goods, and seed patterns in two shades of the same color, may be worn. She should wear few jewels, never pearls around the neck, no earrings, and only a few well-chosen rings.

Sleeves with high shoulders made close at the wrist are most unbecoming to her. She should never wear tight gloves.

Good Taste in Dressing.

It is certain that the question of dress is one of importance, and the woman who affects indifference to it lacks judgment.

A woman who dresses badly loses

half her opportunities, that is, if the defects in her toilet are the result of her indifference on the subject. Mme. de Maintenon asserted that good taste indicated good sense.

It was also she who justly blamed women for overtrimming heavy stuffs, and wearing ill-chosen ornaments. Nothing can be more ridiculous than ornaments out of place. A gown of cheap material, if well made, is often pretty, though simple and unpretentious.

Short, stout women should never wear gowns of rough, shaggy materials. Skirts made of them fall in stiff and ungraceful folds, and the bodies are equally unbecoming.

Dress fabrics in woolen goods should always be soft to the eye and to the touch. China crêpes, colored silks of

medium weight, make charming costumes, and are to be preferred to the
stiff silks; but a black silk gown
should be of good quality, as an inferior grade does not wear well, and
soon grows shabby.

Beautiful feathers are durable and
graceful ornaments for bonnets; cheap
ones are poor economy. Low priced
finery is not worth buying. One should
never economize in this way. It is
never wise to buy one article of dress
noticeably richer than the rest of
the wardrobe. For example, a velvet
dress is serviceable, but unless one can
afford other costumes as elegant, it is
out of place.

Mixed cotton and wool goods are
usually almost worthless. One all
woolen gown is worth two of them.

Pale blue is apt to make blondes look

ashen. Dark blue, on the contrary, is very becoming to them, and a blue velvet gown brings out all their delicate coloring. Neutral tints are very unbecoming to them. Brunettes with an inclination to be sallow will do well to avoid blue, as it makes them appear greenish or tawny. Green is trying to them unless they are very fair. It suits blondes perfectly, especially those who have color.

Pale brunettes should affect shades of red, which increase their beauty. Crimson may be worn by blondes. Yellow is a superb contrast for a pale brunette, especially under artificial light, when it is more subdued than in the sun light. This color softens an olive skin, and borrows from it a creamy tint, harmonizing wonderfully well with dark hair and brilliant eyes. Despite all that may be said, yellow is unbecoming to most blondes.

Only women with beautiful shoulders and arms should wear *décolleté* gowns. Bony necks and arms are certainly not agreeable to the eye, and it is wise to conceal them. But, you will ask, how can one go to dinner, opera, or ball in a high gown? The bodice may be cut low, and the neck and arms covered with tulle or lace. The freshness of a toilet is one of its chief merits, and a new gown should never be worn in the rain and mud. A rainy-day costume is a necessity. Elegant garments should be reserved for visiting and other occasions requiring richness of toilet.

It is absurd to have too many toilets for one season. Everyone knows how often fashions change, and that even a last year's gown sometimes appears almost ridiculous.

A neat suitable morning dress is necessary. Besides this one should have a gown for afternoons at home, a simple street gown, and a visiting costume. This is the minimum of a feminine wardrobe. A clever woman with good taste can at small expense convert her old evening toilets into such as are suitable for home wear. There is no need for me to describe to rich women the costumes for church, weddings, dinners, operas, parties, concerts, balls, etc., and all their accessories.

I may add that diamond earrings are no longer considered good form. Jewels should be worn very sparingly excepting in the evening. Never wear ornaments of any kind over the gloves,

A bracelet is quite as *outré* worn outside the glove as a ring; a diamond
tiara over the bonnet would not be in
worse taste or more absurd. Precious
stones, notably diamonds, worn with a
walking costume, proclaim the vulga-
rian.

GENERAL ADVICE.

MAKING UP.

I DARE not hope that my advice will have sufficient weight with all my readers to induce them to give up the deplorable and disfiguring habit of painting themselves, a habit which as seriously detracts from matronly dignity, as it compromises beauty and youth.

To those who persist, despite my advice, in making up their faces, I will here suggest where to place the paint on the cheek, according to the usage of the eighteenth century.

It should be applied in straight lines, as near as possible to the eyes, as this

layer of carmine increases their brilliancy ; the other three inferior coatings
should be gracefully rounded at an
absolutely equal distance from the nose
and ears, and never extend below the
mouth.*

During the last century, when rouge
was a part of etiquette, and the indication of a certain rank among women,
the court ladies, in all seriousness,
studied the art of coloring their cheeks
in the most aristocratic manner.

They would have been far prettier
still, those charming women, if they
had been content to keep the natural
and delicate coloring of their hedge
rose.

As for enameling ! The enameled
woman must neither smile nor weep
for fear of cracking the ghastly mask.

---

* This may be called the opera-bouffe method, and is not
to be recommended.—II. II. A.

Her porcelain face is cold and expressionless, and her complexion livid in the daytime.

And whitewashes! They are even more fatal to the complexion than carmine. In the name of reason and of good taste, I proscribe them in the dressing room. A resemblance to Pierrot, the clown, is certainly undesirable.

Various Hair Dyes.

I recommend the following harmless dyes to women who object to white hair. Blond hair when turning gray sometimes becomes muddy in color. Strong tea will change it to a light brown. A dye for blond hair may also be made of a strong decoction of brown and oily chicory, which is sold in the form of a sea biscuit in the north of Europe.

Steep iron nails for fifteen days in tea, and you will have a dark dye.

When the hair of the Romans began to grow gray they dyed it in a decoction of walnut. The Persians dyed their hair by using henna daily. The leaves of the henna were reduced to powder, and made into a kind of paste with water. This was applied to the hair, which was washed two hours after the application, when it became a reddish brown, old mahogany. The wash applied again the next morning, with indigo added to the henna, produced a superb black, like the raven's wing.

But I repeat, all anodyne dyes are injurious to the hair, making it stiff, rough and dry.

Dyes made with a base of lead or silver are extremely dangerous. They not only produce baldness, which, alas!

is very common among women in our day, but cause brain trouble and loss of sight, and it seems incredible that a woman will thus endanger -not only her crown of glory, but her most precious sense. Turkish women use a dye which is less dangerous than ours, composed of the soot of incense and mastic rubbed into an odorless oil.

The Greeks have another process which I will describe. It is also less dangerous than many others.

Take sulphate of iron, ten grammes, and Welsh nuts, fifty grammes. Boil the Welsh nuts in three hundred grammes of water, and strain through a cloth. Add the water of the sulphate of iron, and boil again, until reduced to about two-thirds. Perfume and keep in bottles well corked. Apply several times with a fine camel's hair brush.

Remedies for Softening and Strengthening the Skin.

Many of the most widely advertised remedies for softening and strengthening the skin are worse than useless, and are most injurious in their effects. Heroic treatment of the delicate cuticle is neither logical nor to be desired.

Bathing in cold water and friction strengthen the tissues. The stinging sensation of cold water excites the circulation, which is a benefit to the skin. The roughness of skin will sometimes disappear by friction. Rubbing the arms with a hair glove often takes off the down, or at least keeps it on a level with the skin, where it is invisible.

A rough and dry skin may be rubbed to advantage with an emollient. A flaccid skin is sometimes improved by friction with the essence of pimpernel mixed with the essence of rose.

During and After Nursing.

Do not believe those who tell you that your breast will lose its beauty and firmness if you perform the sacred duty of maternity in nursing your child.

During this period, you need for the child, as well as for yourself, a wholesome, sufficiently abundant and well selected diet. Afterward you should continue this régime for a certain time, and under its influence your breast will soon return to its natural roundness and firmness.

Even while nursing you may wear a corset, which will prevent the heavy veins of the breast from distending.

Nourish your child from your own breast. Be sure, that for having sub-mitted with joy to the law of nature, you will remain none the less beautiful and young. The milk which swells the breast should flow into the mouth of the infant. If, while confiding your own flesh and blood to a stranger, you compel the unused liquid to be re-absorbed, you may expect any amount of pain and discomfort and the ulti-mate loss of all form and beauty of the breast; and this is but just, since you have refused to perform the sweet task for which it was destined.

SCENTED WATERS, CONCEN-
TRATED ODORS, POMADES.

Scented Waters.

"Culling from every flower
Their virtuous sweets."

ONLY very delicate and carefully
prepared waters and toilet vinegars
should be used on the face and hands.
Fortunately there are many of these to
be had. Bouquet Katherine is the
queen of scented waters and the reign-
ing favorite at present both in Europe
and America. Such waters may be
usefully applied to other parts of the
body, having the properties of a tonic
for the skin.

I give four recipes for cologne :

First. Alcohol at 30°, 1 quart; essence of lemon, 6 grammes; essence of bergamot, 6 grammes; essence of cedra, 3 grammes; essence of lavender, 1 gramme, 50 centigrammes; essence of neroli, 0 gramme, 50 centigrammes; essence of rose, 2 drops. Stir the mixture well, filter and bottle.

Second. Essence of lemon, 10 grammes; essence of cedra, 10 grammes; essence of bergamot, 10 grammes; essence of fine lavender, 10 grammes; essence of cloves, 10 grammes; essence of rosemary, 4 grammes; essence of thyme, 2 grammes; rectified alcohol, 2 quarts. Mix the essences with alcohol, and filter through paper.

Third. Essence of cedra, 6 grammes: essence of bergamot, 6 grammes; essence of neroli, 1 gramme; essence

of lavender, 1 gramme, 50 centigrammes; essence of rosemary, 1
gramme, 50 centigrammes; essence of
cloves, o gramme, .08 centigramme;
essence of Chinese cinnamon, o
gramme, .08 centigramme; tincture
of musk amber, 1 gramme, 20 centigrammes; tincture benzoin, 6 grammes;
alcohol at 90°, 1 quart. Dissolve
essences in alcohol, filter well.

Fourth. Essence of bergamot, 10
grammes; essence of orange, 10
grammes; essence of lemon, 5
grammes; essence of cedra, 3 grammes;
essence of rosemary, 1 gramme;
tincture amber, 5 grammes; tincture
benzoin, 5 grammes; alcohol at 90°, 1
quart. The alcohol should always be
very pure. Filtering is indispensable.
Cologne improves with age.

The establishment of Jean Farina

keeps it in barrels made of Cedar of Lebanon. Cedar preserves admirably all perfumes, and does not communicate its own odor.

Lavender water can also be prepared at home. It requires: Essential oil, 15 grammes; musk, 2½ centigrammes; spirits of wine, 1 pint. Put the three substances in a quart bottle and shake long and thoroughly. Leave it alone for a few days, shake again, empty into small vials, which must then be hermetically sealed.

Or else: Essence of superfine lavender, 30 grammes; good brandy, 1 quart. One coffeespoonful in a glass of water for toilet use.

The formula is the same for rosemary, with the difference that the thirty grammes of essential oil of lavender are replaced by the same quantity of essential oil of rosemary.

I do not wish to speak of rosemary without revealing its virtues. According to some persons it is believed that the woman who uses it constantly, as a perfume and toilet water, preserves eternal youth. I cannot prove this. It is certain that the rosemary belongs to the family of labiates, and that these plants are reputed to be tonics and restoratives.

The pink has antiseptic qualities which recommend it still more highly for the uses of the body. With its flowers one can prepare an excellent toilet water, of delicious perfume: Petals of pinks, 200 grammes; alcohol at 90°, 1 gramme. Let the petals infuse in alcohol for ten days. After this time, filter through paper, and add a hundred grammes of tincture benzoin.

N. B.—In your preparations never use whisky or wood-alcohol.

Toilet Vinegars.

Under the name of vinegar dishonest tradesmen sell acetic acid. This is dangerous to the skin, which it dries, corrodes, and predisposes to wrinkles. Use cologne, 100 grammes; tincture of benzoin, 20 grammes; good Orleans natural vinegar, 1 quart. Put the cologne and the tincture into a large bottle or jug, then add the vinegar. Let them stand for fifteen days, shaking the bottle every morning. Filter afterward through paper. Prepared filters are found at the druggists.

Although the vinegars for which we give recipes are not open to the

same objections as those sold by un-
trustworthy druggists, they should not
be used too lavishly. A few drops in
a sufficient quantity of water refresh
the skin. The best toilet vinegar
made for sale is the Russian Aromatic Vinegar.

Put no faith in the white vinegars
for any of your preparations.

Here is the formula of a medicinal
vinegar, good for redness of skin and
sores which may appear on the body:
Balm-mint, 27 grammes; spirits of
mint, 25 grammes; spirits of sage, 25
grammes; spirits of rosemary, 25
grammes; spirits of lavender, 25
grammes; Orleans vinegar, 2 quarts.

Lavender vinegar is very easy to
prepare: Rose water, 25 grammes;
spirits of lavender, 50 grammes;
Orleans vinegar, 75 grammes.

Aromatic vinegar is very cheap if one personally gathers the plants: tops of dry absinthe, 40 grammes; rosemary, 40 grammes; sage, 40 grammes; mint, 40 grammes; garden rue, 40 grammes; cinnamon bark, 5 grammes; cloves, 5 grammes; nutmeg, 5 grammes. Let the mixture infuse for fifteen days in one pint of alcohol, then add two quarts of wine vinegar. Filter through paper.

During the flower season, delicious vinegars can be prepared which cost nothing save the vinegar.

Good Orleans vinegar, 1 quart; roses of provins, 50 grammes; hundred-leaves roses, 50 grammes; jasmin flowers, 20 grammes; flowers of fairy queen, 25 grammes; flowers of melilot, 25 grammes; leaves of citronelle, 20 grammes. If dried flowers are used instead of fresh, three pints of vinegar are necessary. Let it infuse for one month, and then filter.

Rose vinegar: Dry petals of red roses, 100 grammes; Orleans vinegar, 1 quart. Eight days of steeping will be sufficient, but the bottle must be shaken from time to time. It should have a large mouth in order to fill it easily. Strain by pressure. Allow it to stand about two days, then filter.

All vinegars made of flowers consist of one hundred grammes of petals, or of whole flowers, and one quart of vinegar.

Virginal milk: Powder of benzoin, 50 grammes; alcohol at 90°, 1 pint; good Orleans vinegar, 1 pint. Put the ingredients in a bottle, and shake each morning. After fifteen days of macerations, filter through paper.

N. B.—Pulverize the powder of benzoin thoroughly with a small quantity
of alcohol and vinegar, so that the
liquid may be clear, then add the rest
of the liquid, stirring continually, and
pour into a bottle.

Concentrated Odors.—Ancient Use of Perfumes.

Perfumes were highly esteemed
amongst the ancients. In the country of the Pharoahs, their use was
carried to excess. The bodies, clothing, tombs, and houses were impreg-
nated with perfumes more or less
agreeable. On feast days perfumed
waters were poured into the streams.

Did not even the Shunamite plunge
her fingers into precious myrrh before
running to meet her spouse? The
Bible is full of allusions to spikenard

and myrrh. The East preserves this love of perfumes.

The Greeks had a certain perfume for each part of the body: Marjoram for the hair, apple for the hands, wild thyme for the neck and knees, etc. They highly esteemed the waters made of the leaves of vines. This mixture of odors could not have been very agreeable.

The ancients invented the pulverizer. Leaders of fashion in Athens conceived the idea of freeing doves which had been bathed in sweet scented waters over the festal board, that the guests might be sprinkled with perfumes from their wings.

In Rome the slaves filled their mouths with perfumed waters and blew them in sprays on the hair of the mistress. In more modern times the perfume was sprayed through an atomizer. The Romans in particular carried the custom of perfuming and living in the midst of strong odors to such an extent, that Plautus exclaimed, "By Pollux! The only woman who smells delightfully is the one who doesn't smell of anything!" Amber and vervain were the favorite perfumes during the latter part of the Middle Ages. In the 13th century women laid away their garments with a certain kind of apple which had a delicious odor. The favorites of Henry III. reveled in neroli and frangipanni. La belle Gabrielle, who reproached her lover for eating garlic, preferred orris and orange flower. Anne of Austria had all her creams and cosmetics perfumed with vanilla.

La Pompadour affected the odors of rose and jasmine.

Choice of Odors.

From a hygienic standpoint sweet odors may be approved of on account of their stimulating and refreshing qualities. Both health and good taste forbid that they should ever be abused. They are not without influence on the temperature and on beauty, especially lavender, lemon, rose, violets, and lilies. It is asserted that they also influence the moral nature. The rose predisposes to delicacy of feeling; geranium to tenderness; lilies to reverie; dark violets to piety; while the white assist digestion. It is said that the woman who loves vervain should cultivate the æsthetic, for her artistic nature is revealed in this choice.

Without carrying the use of perfumes to excess, it is well to select some delicate and light odor. Every woman should repudiate a mixture of odors. She should select her favorite, and remain true to it. All that belongs to her, her books, her stationery, her apartment, the cushions of her carriage (in the 18th century they were stuffed with odorous herbs), her clothing, the least article which she handles, should exhale the same perfume. A great lady once wrote : " The devil may smell of sulphur, I shall smell of orris."

Some people in love with the last century select the Peau d'Espagne.

Russian leather is sometimes considered a perfume. There are women who are content with the delicate odors

communicated from their rosewood
wardrobes. Others perfume themselves with flowers and herbs according
to the season. They begin with violet,
rose, mignonette, etc., with which they
fill their bureau drawers, their pockets
(when their gowns are not in use),
sachets, etc., etc. The odors from
these fresh flowers or herbs, which
fade and die in the wardrobes, are perhaps fleeting, but extremely agreeable.
These women prepare for winter use
the flowers of Melusina, queen of the
meadows, and asperules dried in the
shade. They simply inclose them in
little muslin bags, and put them into
every nook and corner. They suggest the odors of the prairies in
blossom. Our ancestors preferred a
bouquet of odors. They themselves
prepared their sachets. We give the

recipes that those who love a mixture of odors may also be gratified.

1st. Dried leaves of roses and orris,
1500 grammes; powdered bergamot
peel, 250 grammes; cloves and cinnamon, 150 grammes; orange flowers
and clusters of dry acacia, 250 grammes;
powdered starch, 1500 grammes.

2d. Orange powder, 500 grammes;
lavender powder, 50 grammes; benzoin powder, 25 grammes; sandal citron powder, 25 grammes; orange
peel powder, 25 grammes; tonka bean
powder, 10 grammes; clove powder,
10 grammes; cinnamon powder, 10
grammes.

Mix thoroughly. It is not necessary
that the powder be very finely pulverized. If not found at the shops it is
easy to pulverize it at home.

3d. Florentine orris, pulverized, 750

grammes; rosewood, 165 grammes; calamus, 250 grammes; sandal citron, 125 grammes; benzoin, 155 grammes; cloves, 115 grammes; cinnamon, 31 grammes.

The modern perfumer, by the assistance of chemistry, has discovered some delicious odors, from which it is easy to make an excellent choice. A woman of taste always rejects strong or penetrating odors. Her selection is sweet, delicate, light; it charms but never offends.

Sachets.

Sachets are easily prepared. It is only necessary to powder sheets of wadding generously with the perfume selected. These squares are sewed between two pieces of Florence silk and edged with lace, or the powder may be inclosed in little sacks of percaline

or thin silk, and the bag tied with a
narrow ribbon. Sachets for gloves,
laces, handkerchiefs, and silk stockings,
are as easily made as those for wardrobes, bureau drawers, and jewel cask-
ets. It is only necessary to cut them
the proper size. Large squares of
wadded silk may be fastened with ribbons. Many women of taste have
sachets made to fit the drawers of the
dressing-table, bureau, closet walls, etc.
They are of delicate shades of silk or
satin, wadded, perfumed, and tufted
with knots of ribbon.

Thus a delicate perfume is exhaled
everywhere. In the wardrobes and
clothes-presses, skirt sachets are hung
in the skirts. Tiny sachets are man-
ufactured for bonnets, sleeves of gowns,
corsets, each woman confining herself
to her favorite perfume. A delicate

odor precedes her approach. Before recognizing her writing, the odor of the paper betrays the writer. If she loans a book, its perfume recalls the lender and reminds us that it should be returned—or pursues us like a remorse.

Cold Cream.

Oil of sweet almonds, 50 grammes; white wax, 10 grammes; sperm oil, 10 grammes; mix these substances well together, and add rose water, 20 grammes; tincture of benzoin, 5 grammes; tincture amber, 2 grammes.

It may be well to mention that wax and sperm should be melted in a double boiler (Puritan Cooker) to become incorporated with the oil.

Cucumber Cream.

Cut in small pieces one pound of peeled cucumbers from which the seeds have been taken. Add as much of the pulp of melon cut in the same way. Add one pound of pure lard and half pint of milk. Heat in a double boiler for ten hours, without coming to a boil. Strain the mixture through a cloth over a sieve ; allow it to drip and congeal. Wash the pomatum until the water is colorless. Squeeze well into a bag and keep in small jars.

Another recipe : Axonge, five hundred grammes ; cucumber juice, fifteen hundred grammes ; mix five hundred grammes of juice with the whole of the axonge, which must be first softened. When the two substances have been

beaten together for two hours let it
stand until next day, then strain off the
juice, and put five hundred grammes
of it into the lard. Repeat three
times in order to exhaust what remains
of the juice. Melt the pomatum in a
bainmarie on a slow fire for five or six
hours to evaporate the water which
remains in the oil. It should be turned
frequently to accomplish this result.
Beat up the pomatum to make it light
and oily, and then put it in jars.

Glycerine.

All skins, as we have said, will not
bear the use of glycerine. If it
makes the skin red it should not be
used.

Even when it suits the skin it should
never be used pure.*

* The strong affinity of glycerine for water has made it
often most annoying as a healing factor. The first sensa-

Soaps.

Soap is necessary, but care should be taken to rinse the face afterward in soft warm water; use only pure soap. The strong prefumes given soaps are too often only a mask for the impurities they contain. The colors used in soaps (especially rose and green) are dangerous to health and skin. A pure soap should be of a light mastic color and not transparent.

tion produced by an application of glycerine to the tongue is one of burning, almost painful, notwithstanding its sweetness. This burning is caused by the absorption of all moisture from the surface which the glycerine touches, thus drying and parching the nerves. Many women, especially mothers and nurses in charge of infants, are ignorant of this fact, and apply pure glycerine to the tender chafed skin of delicate babies, producing intense pain, which they often attempt to allay by a second application, with only aggravated results. If you have naturally a very moist skin glycerine will not give you this burning sensation. If, on the contrary, your skin is parched and dry, you should not use it.—H. H. A.

Rice Powder.

The rice powder which is sold in the trade is often injurious to the skin. If one could prepare it, it would not only be harmless but excellent for use.

Fill a new earthen jar with six quarts of water and one kilogramme of rice. Let it soak for twenty-four hours, then bottle. During three consecutive days, put in six more quarts of water each day. Let the rice drip on a new hair sieve which must be used only for this purpose. Then expose to the air, protected from dust, on a towel which has been washed in lye. As soon as it is dry, it must be ground very fine in a clean and covered marble mortar. Lastly, sift through a fine white cloth into the jar. Tie the cloth around the mouth of the jar with a tape, and let it sag in order not to lose any of the powder. The jar should have a tight cover.

It is best not to perfume this powder.

When the powder gives out and cannot be immediately replaced, use, instead, the flour of oatmeal, which can be taken up in small quantities on the puff.

If you must purchase rice powder, take care not to select that which is highly perfumed, if the skin is easily affected or irritated. Never leave powder puffs uncovered. They should be kept in very clean porcelain or china boxes.

How to perfume soaps.

Home-made soaps may be perfumed with fine essential oils.

As soon as the mixture is taken from the fire and before placing in molds, stir in the perfume, mixing thoroughly.

A delicious perfume for soap is the juice of raspberries.

For jasmine soap, the perfume of this flower is added. Oil of rose is also very good for this purpose.

PART FOURTH.

PART FOURTH.

JEWELS, CHIFFONS, AND LACES.

Care of Jewels.

Pearls.—Pearls are kept from dying or tarnishing by shutting them up with a piece of ash wood. Let scientific people laugh at this recipe if they will; have faith in the tradition which has been handed from generation to generation in old families. Thanks to this precaution, pearls will never tarnish. This is important to know if one possesses stones of large size and brilliancy, and which may become tarnished in the course of time.

Pearls are easily stained, therefore when buying colored ones it is well to be accompanied by a connoisseur. The lovely Eastern pink pearl strikes the most superficial observer with admiration.

The pink pearl, mounted with white pearls and brilliants, forms the most exquisite ornament conceivable.

The rose pearl of the Bahamas has at first sight a coral tint, but its color is more delicate. It shines and has charming iridescent lights.

The value of a pearl depends upon its form, its smoothness, its size, and its tint. When round, it is called a button. Irregular, it is called baroque.

Anyone who possesses a single row of pearls as large as wild cherries may perhaps be glad to know that in the seventeenth century this string of pearls

was called "l'esclavage de perles,"
and that a locket of brilliants suspended from it was called "boute-en-
train."

It is said of pearls that they presage
tears. But the working woman who
never has owned one surely weeps as
much as the duchess whose jewel
cases overflow with this loveliest as
well as most beautiful of jewels.

Diamonds.—Diamonds should be
carefully brushed with soapsuds and
rinsed in cologne water. When
shaken in a small sack of bran they
acquire great brilliancy.

To discover if a diamond is genuine,
puncture a bit of cardboard with a
needle. Look through the diamond at
the card. If the stone is false you will
perceive two holes on the card. If
the stone is genuine, only one hole

will be seen. Or else place the finger behind the gem and look through the stone with a magnifying glass. The grain of the surface will be perfectly visible if the diamond is false. It cannot be perceived in the genuine.

Through a genuine diamond the setting will not be seen : it is easily perceived looking through a false one.

Precious Stones.—Cut stones should never be wiped after being washed. To cleanse them use a soft brush soaked in soapsuds of pure soap. Rinse and place in sawdust until dry.

Gold Ornaments.—Gold ornaments should be washed in soap water and rinsed in pure water. Cover them with sawdust and leave them for some time. When quite dry, rub with a chamois skin.

Opals.—A Russian superstition has

given this gem a fatal reputation.
The alchemists of the Middle Ages do
not agree with the subjects of the
Czar. They assert that the opal re-
vives the heart, preserves from all poison, all contagion in the atmosphere.
Those who wear it, they add, never
faint, and need not fear heart disease.
The Orientals say that it is impression-
able. It changes color according to
the emotions of the wearer : reddens
with pleasure in the presence of his
friends, and pales before his enemy.

"The ancients," said Buffon, "held
the opal in the highest esteem."
Lovely things have been said of its
changeable tints. "Its lights are
softer than those of the dawn." "It
seems as though a captive rosy ray
trembles beneath its pallor." It has
been called a "moon tear." The

month of October has been dedicated
to it; and those born in that month
should wear it in preference to any
other stone.

I might say a great deal more on the
subject, but I must not forget that I
am merely to suggest how to renew
the opal's polish, when it has been
scratched. Rub it with the oxide of
tin, or mastic (putty) spread on a
chamois skin, and moisten. Polish
with powdered chalk; wash the opal
afterward with water and a soft brush.
If this is done carefully the stone will
not be loosened in its setting.

Silver Ornaments.—When silver fili-
gree ornaments have been blackened
or have lost their polish, they may be
cleansed in the following ways: wash
first in potash water, which must not
be too strong. After rinsing, dip

the articles in a water composed of
one part of salt, one of alum, two
of saltpetre, four of water. Do not
soak longer than five minutes; rinse
in cold water, and dry on a chamois skin.

Or : wash in hot water with a
brush dipped in ammonia and soap.
Rinse in boiling water, and dry in
sawdust. When in the jewel case
they should always be wrapped in
paper.

Dip oxidized silver in a solution of
sulphuric acid, one part; water, forty
parts.

Silver jewelry may also be rubbed
with a slice of lemon, and rinsed in
cold water; afterward wash in soapsuds; rinse again, but in hot water; dry
on a soft towel, and rub with chamois.

Nickel and silver are kept bright by

being rubbed with a piece of woolen cloth saturated in ammonia.

Amber, when tarnished, should be rubbed with pulverized chalk moistened with water; then lay the amber on a bit of flannel and rub with olive oil; dry on a soft piece of woolen goods until the polish returns.

Ivory ornaments are whitened by a solution of peroxide of hydrogen. Expose them to the sunlight in a bath of spirits of turpentine. This produces an excellent effect. Ivory can be cleaned with bi-carbonate of soda. Rub the ornament with a brush dipped in hot water, then sprinkle with the powder.

Care of Furs, Feathers, and Woolen Goods.

Many things and substances are recommended for the destruction of insects.

Pliny says that the Romans used citron to preserve their woolen garments from moths.

In our day, the same insect which destroys furs, feathers, and woolen goods is itself destroyed by the Indian chestnut, cloves, walnut leaves, or common salt.

Generally cedar chips, pepper, or camphor (in large pieces, for when broken it loses strength), are generally recognized as the best preservatives.

Whatever the remedy selected, it is necessary in the first place to shake, beat, and brush the furs carefully (against the grain), and all other articles to be put away when the season is over. They should then be sprinkled with pepper or camphor, and wrapped in a cloth which has been washed in lye water. Close the parcel carefully, and place in a chest into which some insect powder has been sprinkled.

It is well to put away feathers in empty cigar boxes.

If one owns a cedar chest, or closets which are wainscoted with cedar, it is sufficient to hang up the articles after having well brushed and shaken them.

I have seen other methods employed to get rid of moths. A liquor of one quart of alcohol and the same quantity of essence of turpentine, and sixty-five grammes of camphor, is sometimes used. This should be kept in an earthenware jug, and well shaken before using. When the winter garments are put away, soak pieces of blotting paper in the liquid, and scatter among the furs and flannels, which should be rolled up in white cloths. Place one layer at the bottom, one above the article, and one at each side.

Another suggestion: Cover an empty brandy cask on the outside with plaited andrinople. Place the furs and flannels in this, wrapped in white cloths; then replace the cover of the cask, and use it as a table on which to support plants.

If one has neither chest nor cask, after having shaken and brushed the articles, fold them separately in linen paper, sprinkle with pepper and camphor. Roll each parcel in newspaper, do the package up in white cloth, and hang in a closet or dark room.

Clean furs by rubbing them against the grain with heated bran. Use magnesia for white furs.

Cleaning of Lace.

Fine laces should be washed as seldom as possible ; but, when it is necessary, most women prefer to have them
washed under their own eyes. Make
hot soap suds with rain water and glycerine soap. The laces, which have
been rolled on a glass bottle under a
band of linen, are put in the suds and
remain for twelve hours. Renew the
soap suds three times, plunge the bottle
into soft and clear water, and take it
out immediately. The soap which remains serves to give some stiffness to
the lace when pressed by a hot iron.
Pin each point down under a fine muslin, and iron on the wrong side. When
all is finished, raise each flower by a
little ivory stick. Even a duchess is
not above superintending the process

of washing her Argentan, Alençon, or Angleterre laces.

Laces may be bleached by being exposed to the sunlight in soap suds. The points are afterward dried on a cloth to which they are pinned. They are then rubbed carefully by the aid of a sponge dipped in soap suds of glycerine soap. First clean one side, and then the other. Rinse in clear water, in which a little alum is dissolved, to remove the soap.

A little rice water should be passed over the wrong side of the lace with a sponge; then it is to be ironed, and when finished the flowers picked out as in the above method. If the lace is not very much soiled, it can be cleaned with bread crumbs.

As for cream-colored laces, they should be boiled for one hour in soapy blueing water, then taken out and the operation repeated twice, always in fresh water. The third time there should be no blueing in the water, and it should not be rinsed. The lace should afterward be put in gum water, with a little brandy and alum dissolved in it. Then powder lightly with sulphur flour and iron while damp.

Valenciennes should be folded together a regular length, sewed in a sack of fine white linen, and soaked in olive oil for twelve hours. Afterward put some sliced pure soap in water and boil the sack containing the lace for fifteen minutes. Rinse well, dip in a thin rice water, then rip open the sack and pin down the lace to dry Iron it under a muslin cloth.

Black laces should also be folded in a short package and kept in place by stitching at the top, in the middle, and at the bottom. Dip the lace in beer, roll it with the hands, not rubbing too roughly, to clean it. When it is taken out of the beer, press it between the hands without wringing, then roll it in a cloth. Iron it after it has been partly dried, according to the desired stiffness. To iron it stretch it on a thick flannel, and let it remain there. Cover it with a thin piece of muslin to prevent the iron from making it glossy.

When gowns trimmed with lace are put away, cover the lace with silver paper.

To cleanse silver laces and braids, put them in a sack of white linen and dip into one pint of water, adding sixty grammes of soap. Boil well, and rinse in cold water. Apply a little spirits of wine to the tarnished places.

Cleaning and Washing Woolen Goods.

Clean rose-colored cashmere by washing in cold soapsuds. If you attempt to put dye in the water, the material will be spoiled. Rinse well in cold water, and dry in the shade.

To clean white serge, use a decoction of soapwort roots. The gown when washed will be white and soft to the touch. Soap hardens stuff goods, and makes them yellow.

Knitted or crocheted garments should be washed in the following manner: cut one pound of soap in thin slices and melt in a little water, until it has the consistency of jelly. When the preparation has cooled, beat it up with the hand, and add three spoonfuls of grated stag's horn.

Wash the whole material in this mixture, and rinse well in cold water. If necessary dip the articles a second time in salt water to fix the color. Place before the fire ; stir frequently in order to let the dampness evaporate ; be sure not to stretch the articles out to dry.

To clean a faded black cashmere, rub it width by width with a sponge soaked in a solution of alcohol and ammonia, equal parts, diluted with hot water.

Wash merinos and cashmeres in warm water into which Irish potatoes have been scraped. Rinse in good soft water. These materials should not be wrung out. They should be spread smoothly on a line where they may drip, and should be allowed to become partly dry before ironing.

Cashmere may be also cleaned with the water in which Panama wood has been boiled, or in the water of ivy leaves, or in beef gall, which is very good for washing green cashmere. Here is another recipe for black : Rip the garment, carefully taking out threads which adhere to the material. Cover the stains with dry soap. Put one hundred and eighty grammes of mustard flour in six quarts of boiling water, and allow it to boil two minutes longer. Strain through a cloth. Cool the water until the hand can endure it. Put the garment into an earthen vessel, and pour the mustard water over it. Soap carefully, especially the stains; rinse in several waters ; the last should be clear. Stretch on a line. The woolen cloth being dry, cover with a damp cloth to iron. Wash colored

flannel in hot soapsuds. Carefully
avoid rubbing soap on it. Shake
afterward, to get rid of as much water
as possible, and spread it out to dry.
Blue flannel requires bran water without soap. When rinsing, throw a
handful of salt in the water to preserve the color.

The juice of Irish potatoes will remove mud stains on woolen cloth.

It is easy to cleanse at home white
woolen scarfs and shawls. Prepare
soapsuds by boiling good pure soap in
rain water. While the soap is melting
in the water it should be constantly
beaten. Dip the article in the soapsuds, soaking it first in warm and clear
water. Press with the hands without
wringing. Pass through fresh soapsuds; rinse in soft clear water. Dissolve in three quarts and a pint of

water, not too hot, two spoonfuls of pulverized gum arabic. Mix well. When a thick liquid has been obtained, place the article in it and press it well in the hands. Then wring it, first with the hands, afterward in a white towel. Dry it by fastening the whole length to a tablecloth or towel, and covering with another cloth.

Cleaning of Silks.

Silks are easily cleaned if one knows how to work carefully. Mix the following well together. Fifty grammes of honey, as much soft soap, one gill of brandy. Rip the gown, place in cold water, spread on a table, and rub well with a brush dipped in the mixture. Rinse three times in a pail of water, into which sixty-five grammes of gum have been dissolved. Let the garment drip without being wrung, and iron on the wrong side.

Another recipe: Grate five Irish potatoes in clear cold water. If the silk is thin, slice the potatoes instead of grating. Wash them well before grating or slicing. Let the prepared water stand for twenty-four hours before using. Then strain the liquid. Dip the silk in without rumpling it; spread it on a table, wipe both sides with a clean towel, and iron on the wrong side.

Grease stains may be removed either with chalk, magnesia, or ether, or with the yolk of an egg and water. Clean white brocaded silk with bread crumbs. Plain silk requires the following process: Dissolve soft soap in water as hot as the hands can bear;

rub the silk between the hands in the soapy water; rinse in warm water, and dry by pinning on a cloth.

Nothing is so good for black silk, and in fact for many materials, as beef gall. Throw the gall bladder into as much boiling water as you care to use. Spread the material on a table, and with a sponge dipped in the liquid clean the silk on both sides. Rinse in clear water, still on the table, on both sides with a sponge. Dissolve a little gum arabic or gelatine in the water, moisten the sponge with it, and pass it over the wrong side of the silk. Pin the silk on a cloth to dry it.

A good way of removing grease stains from black silk is to rub them very vigorously with a piece of brown wrapping paper.

Silk should never be brushed. The brush ruins it. Wipe it off with a piece of velvet.

Cleaning of Velvet.

A competent maid should understand how to completely renew velvet garments which have been stained, or worn, or have grown glossy. The garment must of course be ripped, breadth by breadth, piece by piece.

Put burning coals in a chafing dish, and place on this dish a platter of thick brass. When it is very hot, cover with a thickly folded cloth dampened in boiling water. Spread on this cloth the velvet, wrong side out. Do not be frightened if you see a black vapor arise. Pass a brush very lightly over the velvet. Let it dry stretched smoothly on a table.

If not to be used immediately, roll it in tissue paper.

When the velvet has been crushed, turn it wrong side out, and hold it above boiling water, exposed to the vapor. Brush it against the grain.

Before putting away gowns, mantles, plush or velvet jackets, the dust should be removed. To do this spread some fine white sand over the material. Brush it until the last grain of sand has disappeared. If mud stains are on the garment, dilute beef gall and a little spirits of wine in boiling water. Wet a soft brush in the mixture, and rub the stain, repeating as often as necessary. Apply to the back of the material a thin solution of gum.

Stains.

A stain is a disgrace to a garment.

It should be removed as soon as perceived.

Ink stains on woolen goods and cloth may be removed with oxalic acid, but that the acid may not injure the material, put strong vinegar over the application. Lemon, milk, the juice of ripe tomatoes, etc., are good for ink stains on white materials.

When the color of a material has been accidentally destroyed by an acid, rub the spot with ammonia, and the color will reappear.

Grease spots caused by dripping candles may be removed by cologne.

Cover varnish and paint stains with butter or olive oil, and then apply turpentine. If the stain is old, use chloroform instead of turpentine, but use it with great care.

Sherry, rubbed in gently, removes stains made by Bordeaux.

Blood stains should be saturated in petroleum, then washed in hot water.

To remove any fruit stain, rub according to the grain of the material and never otherwise.

Grease spots are the most disagreeable stains. They always spread, and are more offensive than others. Fortunately there are many ways for getting rid of them.

Before removing stains on woolen goods, place on them a piece of absorbent paper, pass a hot iron over it, and then use ammonia and soapsuds. Chloroform is successfully used, and also a mixture of alcohol and ammonia. These spots may be also dampened with ammonia water, and ironed under a piece of white paper.

Rub the stain with chalk on the wrong side of the cloth, allowing it to remain on all day. Many persons keep the following preparation to remove stains whenever needed. Make a stiff paste of Fuller's earth and vinegar. Roll into a ball and dry it. To use it scrape the ball on the stain, which must first be moistened; allow it to dry, and then remove the stain with warm water.

Here are three formulæ for removing stains:

First. Essence of turpentine, very pure, twenty-six grammes; alcohol at forty degrees, thirty-one grammes; sulphuric ether, thirty-one grammes; pour into the bottle, cork, and shake well. To use the mixture, place the material to be cleaned on a piece of thickly folded white cloth. Wet the stain thoroughly with the preparation, and rub lightly with a fine cloth. If the stain is an old one, warm the material.

Second. Mix ammonia and ether and alcohol, in equal parts, thoroughly; place on the stain a piece of blotting paper; moisten with a sponge dipped in water, to make it more absorbent; wet it with the mixture; and rub the stain. It will disappear in an instant.

The following will remove a stain of any kind. Pour into a large necked bottle two quarts of pure spring water; add a lump of ashes of old lees of wine, about the size of a nut, a lump of potash, two sliced lemons. Allow this to stand for twenty-four hours. Filter the liquid, and keep in well corked bottles. When you wish to remove the stain, wet it with the preparation, then rub the spot with fresh water.

Odds and Ends.

Wash faded ribbons in cold soap-suds. Rinse, shake out, spread on the ironing board, and cover with muslin, ironing while damp.

Women in mourning frequently discard long crêpe veils and trimmings, not because they are ruined by the rain, but because the maid does not know how to care properly for this material when it is wet. It should be dried immediately, spreading it out, but not near the fire. If it is stained with mud, clean it with cold water, and dry away from the fire, air, and sunshine. English crêpe, when it has become limp, should be dampened with brandy, then rolled on a roller. Moisten it at each turn, and evenly throughout. Milk may also be used to dampen crêpe and to restore its color, but the crêpe should be carefully sponged afterward with water.

Black thread stockings may be washed as follows : never use soap, but a suds made of a teacup full of bran inclosed in a muslin bag, thrown into warm water, and well stirred. First wash the stockings in this preparation. On taking them out of the water, roll them in a towel, pressing strongly, and dry quickly near the fire, not in the air.

If this precaution be taken, the stockings will retain a fine black color, and never grow dingy. If they are neglected and become rusty, the color can be restored by boiling them in one quart of water, into which a few chips of logwood have been thrown.

Felt hats which have been wet
should be brushed before drying. Rip
off the trimmings; begin brushing at
the border, and continue turning, always
on the same side, until the center is
reached at the very top. Place the
hat on a mold and let it dry before
putting it away. It will be as fine and
beautiful as when new.

In putting gowns away for the
season, wrap them in blue paper tightly
sealed. White silk skirts should be
placed in a second covering of muslin,
and the bodices put away in cases or
boxes. Fold the trains their full
length.

To cleanse the collars of garments,
dissolve one part salt in four of alcohol.
Apply with a sponge and rub well.

Cloth, serge, felt hats, may all be

cleansed by dipping a hard brush, which has short hairs, into spirits of ammonia. Rub until the grease spots disappear.

APPENDIX.

APPENDIX.

Stings of Insects.

LIFE in the country has often a drawback in the shape of mosquitoes, whose stings are intolerable. When stung, fly to the garden, get an onion or leek and rub the spot. This treatment is certainly not agreeable, but is most effective. The leaves of vervain will drive away the diligent mosquito. Washing the skin in toilet vinegars and in elderberry water will protect it from these insects. Honey water will calm the irritation. Put one teaspoonful of honey in a quart of boiling water. Use while warm.

Flour applied to the skin dispels

the redness, removes the itching and burning. Another good and easy remedy is to cover the sting with a little moist soap, allowing the lather to dry on the skin.

A solution of menthol in small quantities, in alcohol, is excellent as a lotion, and is good in case of stings of wasps, bees, mosquitoes, or nettles.

Many women use small sticks of cocoa butter as a cosmetic. If two parts of cocaine is added to one hundred parts of cocoa butter, it will produce immediate relief. It is only necessary to rub the spots with the little sticks, and the irritation will diminish.*

If a bee mistakes a rosy lip for a rose, or a white brow for a lily, and if there be nothing near to cure the

---

* Cocoa butter, used on the face, is apt to induce superfluous hair.—H. H. A.

wound inflicted by the busy worker so beloved by Virgil, rub the spot with a handful of parsley. Continue the friction for several minutes.

Chloroform is also prescribed for mosquito bites. It reduces the swelling, and relieves the itching and the slight pain. Ammonia is also excellent.

Headache and Neuralgia.

Oil of peppermint will relieve the awful sufferings of neuralgia. A country doctor recommended plasters of bane-wort to relieve the terrible suffering, and this simple remedy proved very efficacious.

The same practitioner administered a spoonful of common salt as soon as he saw the first symptom of headache. The indisposition disappeared within half an hour. Queen Victoria, who is subject to headaches, has her temples rubbed with a medicated camel's hair brush. Her Majesty is usually relieved of pain within a few minutes.

Inflammations.

Poultices of cooked apples produce good results in cases of boils and inflamed eyelids. Leaves of bind-weed pounded and applied to the boils are also very efficacious.

Insomnia.

To prevent sleeplessness the English have pillows made covered with camel's hair.

Hop flowers and bulbs whose odors are to be inhaled have the same property, and so have onions. Mattresses

filled with pine needles will often induce sleep.

Coryza.

This indisposition comes within our
jurisdiction because it produces ugliness, and makes the sufferer almost
repulsive. Everyone knows the symp-
toms, a red swollen nose, tearful eyes,
a changed voice, convulsions of sneez-
ing, etc. No beauty can withstand it.
In England the vinegar of anemone is
used. Pour a small quantity into the
hand and inhale until it evaporates.

One physician advises salt water
used in the same way several times a
day; others recommend ammonia; a
little camphor taken as snuff sometimes produces good results.

PRACTICAL RECIPES.

Furnished by Harriet Hubbard Ayer.

MANY excellent creams, lotions, cerates, etc., may be prepared at home, if the amateur is willing not only to give her time and patience to the work, but observe exact accuracy in regard to weights and measures, time required for various compounds, etc. To prepare the following formulæ you will require :

Small scales, such as are used by apothecaries ; a mortar and pestle ; a double boiler for the water baths. (I have found the Puritan Cooker, which may be purchased at any of the large house-furnishing shops, the best); a liquid measure, or graduate ; three or four bone or ivory spoons ; a small percolator ; filtering paper ; hair and bolting cloth sieves ; glass funnels.

Perfect cleanliness is absolutely essential, therefore never use utensils which have served for cooking purposes.

Use distilled water only.

424

For Red Hands. (*Berliner Klin.*)

Lanoline, 100 grammes; paraffine oil, 25 grammes; vanilla, 10 centigrammes; oil of rose, 1 drop; apply night and morning.

Lotion for Dry Skin—Wrinkles, etc. (*C. James.*)

Rose water, 200 grammes; milk of almonds, 50 grammes; sulphate of aluminium, 4 grammes. Dissolve and filter. This is an astringent and an excellent tonic for flaccid skin.

Virginal Milk. (*Pol Vernon.*)

Rose water, 900 grammes; tincture myrrh, 10 grammes; tincture appoponax, 10 grammes; tincture benzoin, 10 grammes; essence of citron, 4 grammes; tincture of quillaia; *q. s.* to make an emulsion.

Amandine.

Put into a large marble mortar two ounces of gum arabic and six ounces of white honey; triturate, and when the mixture has been rubbed into a thick paste, add three ounces perfectly neutral almond shaving cream. Then continue the trituration until the mixture has become homogenous. Two pounds of fresh cold pressed sweet almond oil are next allowed to flow from a can above it into the mortar, but only as rapidly as it can be incorporated with the mass ; otherwise, if it enters in too large quantities, the blending is imperfect, and the amandine becomes oily instead of jelly-like and transparent, as it should be when the manipulation has been skillful. The perfume consists of one-half dr. attar of bitter almonds to every pound of the paste. A little attar of rose may also be added. As soon as finished it must be put into earthen jars and closely sealed.

Cold Cream.

Melt three ounces spermaceti, two ounces white wax, and twelve ounces oil of almonds in a water bath ; pour it into a marble mortar, and stir briskly to prevent granulation ; when of the consistency of butter triturate until the mixture has a white, creamy appearance, then, during continued trituration, add drop by drop one ounce rose water, one ounce pure glycerine ; beat for an hour, add ten drops of oil of rose. Put into pots or jars and hermetically seal.

Witchhazel Cream.

One ounce each of white wax and spermaceti, one-fourth pint of oil of almonds, melt, pour the mixture into a marble mortar which has been heated by being immersed for some time in boiling water ; add, very gradually, three ounces of rose water and one ounce of witchhazel ; and assiduously stir the mixture until an emulsion is formed, and afterward until the mixture is nearly cold.

Chapped Hands. (*Monin.*)

Lettuce water, 200 grammes ; pure glycerine, 50 grammes ; tincture of Peru, 15 grammes ; salicylate of soda, 4 grammes ; mix thoroughly, and apply night and morning.

Flushed Face. (*Startin.*)

Orange flower water, 1 quart ; glycerine, 50 grammes ; borate of soda, 10 grammes. Use as a lotion three times a day, applying a little rice powder afterward.

Rough Face and Hands. (*Vigier.*)

Rose water, 100 grammes ; glycerine, 20 grammes ; tannin, 50 centigrammes. Apply a few drops to the hands and face night and morning.

Red Acne of the Face. (*Hillairet.*)

Rose water, 250 grammes ; spirits of camphor, 30 grammes ; powdered sulphur, 20 grammes ; pulverized sénégal gum, 8 grammes. Apply to the affected parts with a small sponge three or four times a day. The little yellow powder which will remain on the face after the lotion has dried should be left as long as possible.

Dentifrice. (*Eau Botot.*)

Green annis, 64 grammes ; cinnamon, 16 grammes ; clove, 1 gramme ; cochineal, 5 grammes ; cream of tartar, 5 grammes ; benzoin or myrrh, 2 grammes ; essence of peppermint, 4 grammes ; pyrethrum, 4 grammes ; alcohol at 80°, 2000 grammes. Bruise all in a mortar, macerate for eight days, and filter.

Cucumber Cream.

Take of oil of sweet almonds, 7 fluid ounces ; spermaceti, 18 dr. ; white wax, 5 dr. ; glycerine, 1 fluid ounce ; green cucumbers, 4 pounds. Cut the cucumbers in small pieces, mash them in a wedgwood mortar, let them macerate in their own liquor for 12 hours, express and strain ; melt the almond oil, spermaceti, and wax together, by means of a water-

bath ; add to it the strained liquor, stirring constantly so as to incorporate the whole together.
Set aside in a cool place (an ice-chest preferred)
till it becomes hard, then beat with a wooden
spoon, so as to separate the watery portion of the
cucumbers from the ointment ; pour off the
liquor thus obtained, and mix the glycerine with
the ointment without the aid of heat, by working it with the hands until it becomes thoroughly
incorporated. Put up in 4 ounce jars, cover
with a layer of rose water, and set aside in a cool
place.

Violet Powder.

Rice flour, 1 pound ; Florentine orris (powdered), ½ ounce ; essence ambergris, 10 drops ;
oil of rose, 10 drops. Mix thoroughly. Sift
through a hair sieve first ; afterward through
the finest bolting-cloth sieve. The mixture remaining in the sieves is unfit for use.

The weights used in this book are practically according to the French standard.

The following comparative tables will give the avoirdupois:

Drachms. dr.	Ounces. oz.	Pounds. lb.	Quarters. qr.	Hundredweight. cwt.	Ton.	Equiv. in Troy Grains.	Equiv. in French Grammes.	Equiv. in minims of pure water at 62°.
1.	⅛ or .125	.0078	...	...	...	54.6875	3.5428	60.
8.	1.	.0625	...	...	...	437.5	28.3424	480.
128.	16.	1.	...	...	...	7,000.	453.4784	7680.
3,584.	448.	28.	1.	.25	...	196,000.	...	...
14,336.	1,792.	112.	4.	1.	.05	784,000.	...	...
286,720.	35,840.	2,240.	80.	20.	1.	15,680,000.	...	...